SEVEN DOWN

SEVEN DOWN

DAVID WHITTON

RARE
MACHINES

Publisher: Scott Fraser | Acquiring editor: Russell Smith
Cover design and illustration: Sophie Paas-Lang
Printer: Marquis Book Printing Inc.

Library and Archives Canada Cataloguing in Publication

Title: Seven down / David Whitton.
Names: Whitton, David, 1967- author.
Identifiers: Canadiana (print) 20210245573 | Canadiana (ebook) 20210245581 | ISBN 9781459748576 (softcover) | ISBN 9781459748583 (PDF) | ISBN 9781459748590 (EPUB)
Subjects: LCGFT: Novels.
Classification: LCC PS8645.H58 S48 2021 | DDC C813/.6—dc23

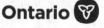

We acknowledge the support of the Canada Council for the Arts and the Ontario Arts Council for our publishing program. We also acknowledge the financial support of the Government of Ontario, through the Ontario Book Publishing Tax Credit and Ontario Creates, and the Government of Canada.

Printed and bound in Canada.

Rare Machines, an imprint of Dundurn Press
1382 Queen Street East
Toronto, Ontario, Canada M4L 1C9
dundurn.com, @dundurnpress ✖ f ⊚

For Jonathan Dewdney

March 11, 2024

Nadja,

Well, here we are, you and me, like the old days, that noxious little office on the corner of Zambak and Istiklal. How did we get anything done? The relentless street hustle, the fossilized plumbing, dust motes streaming through the blinds. All those goddamn cats. Good times, good times.

So we've escaped the "layoffs" once again. Who would have thought it would be us, the last men standing? Would you ever have given odds for such a development? It speaks, I guess, to the soft power of keeping your head down and saying nothing and contradicting no one. The Board has once again invoked the Peter Principle; we have risen to our level of incompetence, like the suckers before us and the dipshits before them. Life is a continuum. And while I'm grateful to be able to make my mortgage payments, it also means that every single moment of my workweek is an affliction.

Here are those interviews you wanted, all the civilian assets we burned in Operation Fear and Trembling, compiled for your convenience in one slim blue binder. I've had a chance to listen to some of the tapes, and from what I can tell, these transcripts are solid product. Someone said once that life can only be understood backwards, but must be lived forwards. So it is with these accounts. You'll notice that I've arranged them out of chronological order, and also out of the order in which they were filed, but, I hope you'll find, to some poetic effect. Pay close attention, therefore, to the date on each transcript.

Like everything else related to the operation, this binder has been a nightmare to assemble. The interviews were conducted over a two-year period, with the last one, incredibly, taking place a little over five weeks ago. Why, you ask? Because we lost that particular contractor. No, I'm not shitting you. One of the asset coordinators lost her contact details, and no one in the department could remember where she'd been placed, or if she'd even existed. I am deeply embarrassed for us, Nadja. You know my thoughts on this.

There were too many points of failure. Whoever designed the operation — Berger and his sycophants? this stinks of them — failed to account for the unaccountable. Just read the transcripts; even our assets understood it, and they knew screw all about what was going down. Humans are little whirlwinds of chaos. We who have transcended humanity can laugh at them all we want, but we depend upon their labours and must respect their fearful power.

Here's a story for you. A few years ago, I decided to go back and visit the city I grew up in. It's not close to here, took some doing, connecting flights, et cetera et cetera. I'd had a happy childhood there, and a rowdy but good-natured young adulthood. My parents were solid and kind and they let me Be, in the Platonic sense. They let me become the person I was destined to be, for better or — actually, just for worse. In my teenage years I had fine girlfriends and a cohort of chums who I understood and who understood me. I was something of a bohemian, I'm not ashamed to say; I took psychedelics and listened to dissonant music. I had drunken dalliances in the alleyways outside of rock clubs, I aspired to become a painter in the mould of the great Basquiat. The city was burnished in my mind, a peaceful beginning to an otherwise somewhat brutish life. And particularly in later years, as I progressed in my career, and saw and did the things I saw and did, this place and the person I was inside it took on an outsize importance. I longed to return to it. So, a few years ago, in the wake of some professional embarrassment or another, I went back, what the hell, and strolled the streets and sidewalks of a city that still felt so unresolved to me. I walked past the downtown movie theatres that I'd snuck into when I was a kid, where I'd seen *Red Dawn* and *Cheech and Chong* and *Superman II* — I forget all the pictures I saw, there were so many — but the point is that those flickering palaces in which I'd whiled away all those afternoons were long gone, demolished, or else turned into "event spaces" or internet cafés. I walked past the old library, a handsome limestone edifice that would soon be gutted so that a tower of condominia could rise from its innards like a great glass dildo. Eventually I worked up the nerve to undertake a pilgrimage to my old neighbourhood, to the house where I'd grown up, those endless summer days riding my bike through the parks and trails, the winters spent sledding down the slopes of a disused quarry. But I found, after I got there, that my childhood home had been torn down, erased, replaced with a weed-strewn metered parking lot. The blue spruce in the front yard, gone. My dad had planted it the day I was born.

We long to return to a prior state, Nadja, one of innocence — but that state is forever gone, if ever it existed, and if we wish to press on, we must radically accept the new reality: of grand Victorian houses razed for parking lots, of toy stores turned into strip clubs, of golf courses cutting through endangered Carolinian forests. The world is on fire, Nadja, and humanity has gone insane. We must find a way to be good with that.

Enjoy the attached.

OPERATION FEAR AND TREMBLING
ASSET DEBRIEFINGS — MARCH 7, 2022
TO FEBRUARY 3, 2024
Compiled by N. Osterberg for Presentation
to the Board of Directors
Pre-Board and Board Meetings
March 18, 2024 | San Diego
Sheraton Hotel Conference Room A

CONTENTS

**ASSET ID: "RESERVATIONS" [Legal name Summer Johnson]
MARCH 8, 2022 — 21:04 GMT**

1 day after Operation Fear and Trembling

[Preliminary comments redacted.]
—I was unwell, yes. I was shivery, nauseous, my brain throbbed behind my eyes. A stomach bug, I thought at first, before my self-diagnosis grew more ominous. I couldn't, though, I just couldn't let my mind go there. And then of course, me being me, it did anyway. Why do women vomit in the mornings? I couldn't allow myself to consider it. That I might be, fuck. Not now, not now, it would be so unfair. I've been mostly careful, all this time, with Steve, we almost always use raincoats. I'm sorry, you said you wanted everything. Is this, am I oversharing? You said you wanted details. And also it's important that you understand, I guess, the ordeal that you ... that I endured. As if the situation weren't bad enough, I had contracted some kind of norovirus, or else I was ... plus it was a Monday, the timing was so awful. Plus Steve and I had stayed up late the night before, mostly drinking, but also ... being intimate, so I was hungover and underslept. That really didn't help, believe me.
—So, if we could maybe skip any extraneous —

—Actually, I don't believe these details are in any way extraneous, because, if I may? Because it's important you understand the sacrifices I've made. It doesn't diminish my regard for, it doesn't mean I'm not happy that I, plus maybe, if I might? For the sake of the next person, you'll stop scheduling these things on a Monday, when people maybe are statistically more likely to be hungover and underslept and feeling vulnerable? I'm sorry. That was, that was not called for. I'm, where was I?

—Your description of the day of the operation. It was 5:15 in the morning.

—It was 5:15 in the morning, yes, thank you. I'm front of house, I work the morning shift, seven to three, so I wake up with the birds. Steve was still in bed, he wouldn't get up for another couple of hours. I was standing at the kitchen counter, trying to tamp down the bile with a fruit smoothie.

—Nice. What kind of fruit?

—Here we go again. What does that have to do with anything? Why would you care? It was a guava-pineapple concoction, mixed with yogurt. It helps me digest, if that's important for you to know. It helps me go to the bathroom. Sorry, sorry. I imagine you must be recording this. That thing in the ceiling, it's a device? A microphone? Okay. Sorry. I'm just tired. I don't know how to feel right now. I didn't expect you to be handsome. You people, in my mind you all look like sixty-year-old tax lawyers, but your hair, it's so wavy, it's almost distracting.

The light outside. On Monday. It was that odd predawn blue black. The light inside was warm and yellow and it was so comforting I considered calling in sick. Coffee was steeping in the Bodum. The smell of that, the aroma … And I felt an intense grief for the morning I wouldn't have, you know, reading a book in bed, sipping coffee, next to Steve.

—Right, again I'll remind you that —

—Just, if you could give me a moment, [Redacted]? May I call you [Redacted]? I'm setting a scene.

—*Please make it brief.*

—Okay, so. Intense moment of grief. I rode it out. Then, staring at nothing, a souvenir magnet on the fridge of the San Jacinto Aerial Tramway, Palm Springs, California, I remembered that I was forgetting something. What was it? My morning routine was smoothie, coffee, and then, what was it? Oh yeah, Twitter, I had to check Twitter. I picked up my phone, hit the app. I've been doing this for so many years it hardly serves to call it a habit; it's a lifestyle by now. I refreshed my Twitter feed and, per my ritual, scrolled backwards. It's a way of putting it off, the inevitable, I suppose. I could have just gone straight there, to the account, but you can imagine how —

—*I'm sorry, which account is this?*

—The account that you guys made me follow. Unfavorable semicircle, it's called, with an at sign in front of it. You really don't know about it?

—*Not my department. Go on.*

—Well, you can imagine how it terrified me. Every day I was like, what would I see there, what phrase or aphorism or gibberish would @unfavorablesemicircle spew into my feed? Mostly I follow celebrities — Miley Cyrus, Lizzo, some stand-up comedians. The odd news account. Dril, of course. And sometimes I get sucked in, all the bickering, every day there's a scandal. But inevitably, in the middle of all my slack-jawed scrolling, there would be this live hand grenade in the form of @unfavorablesemicircle, which blew it all up. Sometimes I wouldn't even realize I was reading one of your tweets, I was so glassy-eyed. I'd read something like "The greatest hazard of all, losing oneself, can occur very quietly in the world" and think, Jesus, Miley's off her meds, and then snap to and see your stupid username and my reverie would be ruined, I'd be back in my kitchen with my goddamn phone.

But after that I'd look around, at the fridge magnet, the coffee maker, Steve's bottle of CBD oil on the counter by the microwave. And I'd become, I don't know. Happy, maybe. The world, no matter how shit the weather, no matter how toxic the morning's news, the world would just sparkle, you know? Whatever it was that would one day be required of me, whatever important or terrible thing, it wouldn't be today. Today was a bonus day. That's how it felt to me.

Last Monday, though … god, last Monday? Yesterday, I mean. Yesterday I stared at that black slab in my hand with horrified disbelief. It was the trigger phrase, written in light on the screen of my phone. As if somehow my fear of those words had called them into existence, and if only I could calm down they would disappear back into the pixels. I shut my eyes … one, two, three, four … opened them. And tried again. And still they were there, those words: "I stick my finger into existence and it smells of nothing." Today was the day of the operation. I was not hallucinating. "I stick my finger into existence and it smells of nothing," said @unfavorablesemicircle. Again I rejected this, I groped around for other plausible explanations. Someone somewhere could have pushed the wrong button. Why not? A quick check-in with Regional would clear it up, they would reassure me and send me on my way, which, a normal shitty day at work? Was looking pretty great right now.

It was maybe a minute. Maybe less. Maybe more. When it hit me. The trigger was real, it was not a mistake. I … I managed to make it to the kitchen sink before I barfed up my smoothie.

—*Do you need to pause for a bit? Would you like some water?*

—No, no, I [inaudible].

—*That's fine. Take your time.*

—I tried to breathe. A three-part breath, expanding the stomach, then the ribs, then the clavicle. The kitchen was vibrating, I couldn't get it to stop. I tried to think. *Laptop*, I thought then, per my training. In times of stress your thinking becomes primal. Go to laptop, Summer. Get laptop. I didn't move. I stared at my coffee mug. My poor little coffee mug, waiting for me by the Bodum. Steve had brought it home from Newfoundland. It had Viking sod hut dwellings on it in gold embossed lines. My heart was busy breaking, looking at this mug, when along came my second thought. Today is the day, went the thought. This is what it's all been about. Today is the day. And I didn't know whether to be terrified or relieved. You didn't have the decency. You didn't tell me what to expect, what it was that I was supposed to do. But I guess you couldn't, could you?

—*Was that a, I'm sorry, was that a rhetorical question or …*

—I'm asking.

—*Ma'am, I'm in Quality Assurance. I have no insight into Operations.*

—No, of course not.

—*So please, if you could just …*

—Continue. Okay. I keep the laptop in a Company-issued lockbox. I keep the Company-issued lockbox in the basement, under the stairs, under a pile of old blankets. Regional has the combination. When they clear out my things, they'll find it there. So anyway, what happened next was I dug out the laptop, went to YouTube. This was five, maybe? Minutes? If that? After my discovery? I'd rinsed the vomit from my mouth and run downstairs. But it wasn't necessary to rush, because you made me wait there like, fifteen minutes, kneeling on the concrete, refreshing the YouTube feed, praying that Steve wouldn't wake up early and find me.

Finally the feed reloaded and a new video appeared. "DOWN7," it was called, like a stock market symbol. I hit Play.

It was a low-resolution video, black and white, nothing much to it, just pixelated palm trees bending in a thunderstorm, punctuated by bursts of static. The audio made my skin crawl. You couldn't have chosen creepier music, could you? It was like a song from an ice cream truck, far away, full of chimes and bells, childlike and squelching, like a broadcast from an old-timey shortwave radio.

Not that I understood what I was watching. Not yet. I was in a thoughtless panic, unable to even try to remember what I was supposed to be doing. But after a moment, after several moments of staring at nothing, I regained myself and applied my attention to the task at hand. I downloaded the YouTube video and opened the file with OpenPuff.

—*I'm sorry, OpenPuff?*

—The program? That came with my laptop? It decodes things. It decoded the YouTube video and found the image you'd hidden inside it.

—*Is that right? Clever.*

—You don't know about the hidden image?

—*I'm Quality Assurance, not IT.*

—You really don't have any idea, do you, what the others in the Company are doing.

—*It's a sandboxed work culture. There are reasons for that.*

—Uh-huh. Well. Anyway. After my moment of staring in thought-less panic at nothing, I came back to myself and remembered what it was I was supposed to do in this circumstance. Hidden inside the swaying palm trees was a second image, a what-do-they-call-it. Like an old portrait that's been painted over. What do you call it? Anyway, a second image, it was there all along except you couldn't see it unless you had the software to decode the jpeg. The second image was — pentimento. That's the word.

—*I'm sorry?*

—The picture that's hidden beneath another picture.

—*Ah. Yes.*

—The second image was a postcard, a faded photo of a canal with a sailboat moored on its bank. On either side of the waterway, a line of picturesque rowhouses, brightly painted. In the top left-hand corner, in that funny bulbous script that old postcards always used, the words *Greetings from Copenhagen*. And at the bottom, handwritten in blue ink, were the words *The gardens are verdant*.

—*This was the, I assume, the handshake?*

—The what?

—*Sorry. It's a term of art. A verbal confirmation. An unlikely exchange of words. It's a way for an operative in the field to confirm that you are you and he is him.*

—Okay. Well —

—*I'm surprised they didn't mention the term in your training.*

—Okay. Well, they didn't. But I understand the concept. Such a simple thing, you know? A bland thing, even. Dumb, even. Such a dumb, bland, simple thing, and yet so ominous. Greetings from Copenhagen. The handshake, sure. This was the sentence you gave me. But why? I always wondered about that. Why me, I mean. What you saw in me. Originally, I mean, all those years ago. Maybe my anger? Was what you saw? Because there was nothing special about me. Or maybe it was my lack of … my aimlessness. My lack of belief. In anything at all.

I wiped the hard drive, wound up the cords, and packed it back into the lockbox. And this is the part, I suppose, where I tell you that the laptop was sobbing.

—*Pardon me?*

—You said you wanted to know everything. So here it is. The laptop was sobbing. I stopped all of my packing. I was … not alarmed, not exactly. Confused, I guess, with an undertone of abject terror. Tears ran down the length of the laptop, great gobs of snot dripped onto the concrete. But then, of course, I realized the sobs were coming from me, those horrible animal noises from my own wretched throat, and the realization somehow made everything all the more dire. I was unwell, remember. The laptop was slimed with my sinus fluids. I picked it up and mopped it with the sleeve of the super-comfy turquoise terry cloth robe that I will never see again, and placed it back inside the lockbox, and placed the lockbox under the stairs, and buried it under the blankets, and went upstairs and got dressed and applied my makeup as if it were just any old day. And when the time came, I tiptoed into the bedroom and kissed Steve on the lips. He grunted, he said, "What the hell, Summer," and I told him how much I loved him, and told him how lucky I was to have such a sexy, sensitive, thoughtful man in my life.

Do you have any of those in your country, I wonder?

—*Let's leave it there for a moment, if you don't mind? Can I get you anything? Coffee? Pretzels? There's a machine down the hall.*

—No, I'm fine. I'm fine.

◆ ◆ ◆

March 8, 2022 — 21:51 GMT

—*Sorry about that. I just had a — There was a thing I had to take care of.*

—That's fine. It gave me time to check my messages.

—*Your ...*

—Kidding. You guys took my phone, remember?

—*We did?*

—Uh-huh. So I can't help but wonder, will you issue me a new one? Or is that not going to happen? Are you really going to make me walk around in the year of our Lord 2022 without TikTok?

—*I'm making a note to ask someone. I can't guarantee any immediate, uh, satisfaction, however.*

—I'm willing to delay my satisfaction if at some point in the next month I can start watching nonstop dance-offs and street goofs.
—*Could we, uh* …
—Yes, certainly. I'm sorry.
—*Continue with yesterday?*
—Sure.
—*You were saying. The stress you were under.*
—Stress, yes, sure. Naturally. But something else, too, something somewhat harder to explain. A part of me, I guess, just a small part, had been looking forward to yesterday. If I'm being honest. I knew I'd lose all of it, everything, my whole world, but this tiny little part of me didn't even care, for real. Wanted it, even. It wanted me to lose everything, if only because that might feel like a satisfying conclusion to the last seven years. How odd is that? I'd actually been looking forward to this day, but now that it was here, I … What is wrong with me? Sorry, I, just a second, I.
—*I can get you some tissue.*
—No, it's okay, I'm better, I'm better. Where were we?
—*Your morning.*
—Right, so. Greetings from Copenhagen. I couldn't stop the words from worming their way through my brain. Greetings. From. Copenhagen. Around and around through the grey junk, till I was so muddled I couldn't perform the simplest of tasks. I'd been waiting for this day for so long, you understand, and I had literally no idea what I was supposed to do. Can you imagine the anxiety? Not to know what it is that you must do? Not to know if you're capable even of doing it?

I was on front desk, people were saying words at me, I did my best to make sense of these globules of sound. The phone would ring, I would flinch. "Good morning," the phone would say, "I'd like to reserve a room for the twenty-fifth." And I would nearly sob with gratitude. All the phone wanted was a room. Just an innocent request for a room. At 10:30 a.m., on break, I called my mom. "Hi, Mom," I said. "Oh hello, Summer," she said, "this is a surprise." "Why is it a surprise?" I said. "Well," she said, "you never call from the hotel. You are at the hotel, aren't you? Is everything okay?" "Sorry, Mom," I said, "I meant to call yesterday, but things got crazy." There was a short but significant pause, then she said, "You sound funny, dear."

I stared then, for a second, at the staff room wallpaper, the flocked green stripes on the matte green background, and wondered at all the effort that went into that crappy generic wallpaper — it was some Glidden wallpaper designer's project for like six months — and with a force of will I had never suspected myself to possess, I stopped myself from collapsing.

"Funny?" I said. "I'm sorry, I was just wondering how dad's scoping thing went. His barium thing. That was last week, wasn't it?" Mom snickered. "Oh, it was fine, you know, but the barium part was miserable. You've never seen such an old grump."

When the phone call was done, I rushed to the restroom and, should I redact? No? Fine, I have no boundaries anymore, anyway. I vomited into the toilet, with violence. Sorry. I used to have boundaries, but I no longer care where I end and where others begin. Per my training.

—*Maybe not every single detail is necessary.*

—Yes, okay. Sorry. I'm just … never mind.

As the day wore on, I only felt worse. This was a surprise. I'd thought I'd feel better, reconciled to it, you know, like destiny fulfilled, but I felt only dread. Some elemental part of my brain was performing my tasks. Some carnivorous lizard cranking the levers that worked my arms. Several times I bolted from the desk to stress-pee in the staff toilet. "You look pale," Addilyn said.

—*One second. Addilyn?*

—No, I've told you about Addilyn. Anyway, I told someone. The colonics? Who gets all the colonics? She was in the restroom, smoothing her hair in the mirror. "Hangover," I told her. "My kind of Sunday," she replied. And my mind flashed on Steve, an image of Steve, he'd still be in bed, hugging my pillow, and this thought was so painful I couldn't catch my breath.

You're so stupid when you're young, you believe such stupid things. You make such stupid decisions. Maybe you're angry. Maybe the soft artistic boy you thought you'd marry has just cheated on you with some waif who makes candles for a living. Maybe you don't care anymore, about this trash city and all the idiots who populate it. So you do something rash, out of spite. You think there's no way you'll regret it, but then seven years pass, and you meet Steve, Steve the sexy social worker, always nicks his chin when he shaves, and everything changes. But by then it's too late, you're not allowed out. You're trapped in the decision you made when you were young and spiteful and stupid. So, but, you know. What is life if not regret? At 1:45 p.m., I answered line two. The phone burbled, and my hand shook so violently I couldn't keep the receiver on my ear. "Good afternoon," I said. "King William Hotel." The slightest of pauses, and I knew somehow, deep inside me, what was coming next. "Greetings from Copenhagen," the voice said, male. A male voice. "The gardens are verdant," I managed to reply. "Convention floor women's facilities," the voice said, "middle stall, thirty minutes." The line went dead. I set down the receiver, looked out at the lobby. It was speckled with these tiny white stars. And behind the stars, all those people going about their day. Travellers with Lonely Planets tucked into their pockets. I wanted so badly to be one of them. Business people grinning, grim-faced, shaking their shitty hands. Conventioneers with lanyards round their necks, staring at their literature. The white stars multiplied, grew brighter, buried all those people under their celestial light. Addilyn's voice came from somewhere. "Summer?" she said. "Are you all right? You look like you're about to —"

But I didn't hear the rest. I was gone, out, I was somewhere else. I was walking through a tunnel. I was dreaming, reliving a memory. It was dusk, the blue hour, and the end of the tunnel was glowing. It was two weeks ago, the ass end of February. There had been a thaw, and then rain, and then a refreeze, so that everything outside was silvery ice. It was one of those bike tunnels that runs under railway berms. Orange-tiled walls, pigeon turds on the ground. Mona was waiting halfway. She didn't say hello. First thing she asks is have I been eating. "No, Mona, no, I haven't been eating," I say, heavily sarcastic. "Yes, I've been eating. Jesus." She says, "It's important that you take care of yourself, you know. Have your periods levelled off?" "I still get crampy," I say, "but the prescription has helped, thank you." She peers into my eyes. "Are you having sex?" "Oh god," I say, "I don't know." I'd been seeing Steve, and I really didn't want the Company to find out. "It's an important part of life," Mona says. "It helps with the stress. If you can't find a sex partner on your own, we can arrange for a professional." I gave her one sharp nod to indicate that this discussion was over, told her I'd keep it in mind. Then she handed me the package for March and smiled the way she always smiled, not the tiniest indication that this would be the last time we met, and she turned and left, her funny little Hush Puppies echoing against the concrete. I waited five minutes per protocol, then walked the other way, and when I came out the end I was slumped in a chair in a room with green flocked wallpaper. Addilyn was kneeling in front of me, stroking my hand. Our supervisor stood behind her in his smart navy suit, holding a glass of water. His desk was to the left, two framed diplomas on the wall. I looked around, confused. It was his office. "Oh, thank god," Addilyn said. "You're back."

"What time is it?" I managed to say. She checked her wristwatch. "It's 1:55. You've been out for a while." "Okay," I said. "Okay, okay." I wobbled upright. "Whoa, whoa," Addilyn said, "where do you suppose you're going?" "The ladies," I said. "I have to go to the ladies." And then I stumbled off. And yes, before you say anything, I fainted, I did. And yes, it's as unnerving to me as it is to you that seven years' work could be flushed away so easily. Flushed away. Sorry, bad joke. Where was I.

—*Your contact directed you to the convention floor women's facilities. Where are they located?*

—On the convention floor. Excuse me, are we, is this an airport? I thought we were in an airport, but maybe not. That blindfold on the car ride over here? Was a bit of overkill. Like, you trust me enough to carry out your little operation, but you don't trust me not to spill the beans on where your interrogation room is? I don't even have a phone.

—*Just following the manual. You know how much we love procedure.*

—Fucking bullshit. And it's so damp in here. And fluorescent. It feels, what's the word? It feels down in the ground. Subterranean. How far down are we?

—*Yeah, so I'm not, uh, free to discuss anything other than your, uh, narrative.*

—Uh-huh, sure, sure. Sorry. The, uh, the convention floor women's facilities. They're on the convention floor, just to the east of the Imperial Room. And they're strictly off-limits to staff, not that that's ever stopped any of us. A few years ago all of the guest facilities were remodelled to look like they came from some high-end Victorian spa, all white tile and marble, waterfall faucets and champagne-coloured hand linens. It's a lovely place to do your business, however vile.

There are five stalls in there. I entered the middle stall, per instructions, dropped the toilet seat cover and sat, and if I'd been able to think straight, I suppose I might have thought about my new life, what it would look like, my new friends in my new country, my new esteem, my new money. I doubt very highly I would've thought about my old life. I doubt my heart could have taken that kind of strain. I was moving forward through the tunnel now, no looking back. At 2:15 p.m., I heard the restroom door open, the clack-clack-clack of heels on tile. Then nothing. Whoever it was had stopped near the sinks. I held my breath, waited. But there was no approach. In a moment, the heels retreated, the door opened and closed, and I was alone once again.

I glanced at my watch. It was 2:16. My contact was late. I thought through the protocols for a situation like this, but the only one that came close was 7.1, Abort Operation. This felt extreme, who knew what had happened? Maybe there was a miscommunication, maybe my contact was stuck in an elevator, anything was possible, so I held on a little while longer, and in a few minutes was rewarded with the door opening again, more footsteps. And this time a pair of black patent mid-heel pumps appeared under the stall door. After a moment's hesitation, a tiny manicured hand reached under the door and pitched a sleeved key card onto the floor.

I knew that hand. I'd seen that manicure.

It was Ivy from Systems. Just a few days before, she'd gotten a metallic periwinkle shellac mani — so fun. When you work front of house, you're only allowed a basic nude. I was always so jealous of her options. I'd met her at the staff party three or four Christmases ago; we'd made fun of the karaoke morons, mostly people in Management. I was ... well, I couldn't believe it. She's a nice person, if a bit ... intense, maybe, maybe a bit clingy. Married, one kid — a boy. We'd hung out a few times over the years, I babysat her son when they needed a date night. She'd been at the hotel even longer than me, loyal, took her job seriously. I never would have guessed. She'd seemed so happy. But maybe I'd seemed happy, too, right? You never really know a person. I mean fuck, honestly, you never know yourself. I wanted to say something to her, like, Oh, so hey Ivy, what the hell were you thinking? Was it a guy? Some guy you threw away your life for? But of course I said nothing.

The hand disappeared. But the shoes remained, still pointed toward me. There was a pause, a very pregnant one. For a second it felt as if she might say something, a disclosure, a what, an instruction of some sort, an offering of wisdom, but after an endless moment, the shoes finally pivoted and clacked away.

The poor woman. I still think about that party, I don't know why. Do you have Christmas parties in your country?

—*Is that a serious question?*

—I'm sorry. I'll try, I'll try to be more, I'll try to be succinct. I pulled the card from the sleeve. Attached to the card was a sticky note. *Spoil or Destroy*, it said on the top side. I flipped it. *If you marry*, it said on the back, *you will regret it. If you do not marry, you will also regret it*. I tore up the note and flushed it and left the stall and washed my hands and took a moment to stare at the lunatic in the restroom mirror. The hand soap there was bergamot, a gorgeous scent. I put my fingers to my nostrils and inhaled, and for a second I felt calm.

My mother's garden, the back patio, the lawn chairs and bird calls. The greasy funk of the charcoal grill. The squirrels gambolling along the telephone wires. I felt okay. I'd prepared for this. All this stuff, these smells and sounds and pictures, all of my old life, it would all be up there in my head. It didn't matter where I went.

—*Could we ... could we just take another ...*

—Sure, no problem. Take as long as you need.

◆ ◆ ◆

March 8, 2022 — 22:30 GMT

—*My apologies once again. Now, I think when we left off, we were talking about the key card?*

—The other one who was here. The tall one. A couple of hours ago. He said his name was [Redacted]. I'm wondering if he'll come back. Not that I don't like you, it's just, I was thinking, if he wanted some company for dinner tonight, I'd be. I'd be available.

—*[Redacted]? He's married.*

—Of course. I'm sorry. I'm just so thirsty. It's a stress response. The key card, yes.

So this whole time, Addilyn, the one who gets all the colonics, had been filling in for me on front desk. No complaints, not from Addilyn, she's such a sweetie. When I relieved her she gave my arm a little squeeze and said, "It's just a job, darlin', you don't owe them anything." Which, in a way, you know, was the worst thing she could have said, because it made me almost sob with gratitude. She's such a lovely person, and I felt weirdly like somehow I'd betrayed her. Anyway. I returned to my station and waited for what came next. Those final few minutes of the afternoon were a blur of voices and faces and smiley smiles and bland platitudes. Good afternoon, ma'am, how might I make your day better? Of course, I'd love to help you with that. Could I just see some photo ID, please? Enjoy your stay. But as the seconds ticked by, these interactions grew more dreadful. My shift ended at three, and as three drew closer, every face took on more potential.

Then, at 2:45 or thereabouts, a surprise. Or rather, a commotion. A reverberating crash, metallic, not like gunfire, not like explosives, but the sound of something going badly wrong. A woman screamed, followed by a chorale of frightened voices all around me, crying out, exclaiming things. I startled from my reverie, peered out into the lobby. A man in royal-blue coveralls was hanging from the giant chandelier in the middle of the lobby floor. It was one of the Engineering staff; I couldn't tell which, his back was turned to me. He was rocking back and forth; his ladder had dropped out from under him and he was thrashing his legs through the air in some vain attempt to keep himself from falling.

I stood there, rubbernecking, what else could I do? I was trying to understand what it was that was happening, when a person appeared at the counter in front of me.

"Uh, hello, sir," I said. "I apologize for the tumult."

Did I actually say *tumult*? Did I use the word? Tumult? Probably I said something else.

I don't know that I even looked at him. If I did, I barely registered it. He was medium height, I think, and medium build, with medium-brown hair. He wore a pinstripe suit.

"If you marry," he said, "you will regret it. If you do not marry, you will also regret it."

They say that when you're frightened, you jump out of your skin. In my case, the dissociation was greater than that. I felt my mind float out the back of my head and hover like a drone. I watched myself stiffen, my eyes dart wildly back and forth like a pressure gauge as I attempted to process the moment, until, finally, I remembered to pick up the room card. It was sleeved and sitting by my right hand. Steadfastly avoiding any glimpse of his face, I offered it to him. "Enjoy your stay," I said.

He snatched the card without a word and headed toward the elevators, while a crowd murmured around the chandelier.

My heartbeat. I won't describe my heartbeat. I won't describe my bowels or my throat or my armpits or my crotch. No extraneous details, I understand. I wish I could say I had the presence of mind to take a deep breath, take one last look around this place that I'd spent so much time in, acknowledge the end of my old life, the beginning of the new. But I was in a state of extreme agitation. This was it. It was done. It was done. It was done. I turned from my terminal, retreated into the backroom, grabbed my coat and purse from a peg by the coffee station, and proceeded out of Reservations, past the staff lockers, toward the emergency exit. I remember … I remember looking up … and oh, here's a detail,

I remember looking up and seeing the closed-circuit camera and thinking, they must have someone in Security.

The air outside was cool, too cool. Gelid, the word I think is. Gelid, yes. A crossword word. It blew through the fabric of my skirt, bit at my skin. To my left, a green garbage bin radiated rotten produce. Two pigeons in the alley were fighting over parmesan truffle fries. And then suddenly that was it, it was over, I was free.

Seven years I'd been waiting. Not quite the ending I'd been hoping for. Not that that matters, of course. My feelings are inconsequential, it's the plan that's important. I am no more than a replaceable part, a clutch, a shock absorber; I am not the car. I started walking. I clamped my arms across my chest and hustled down the alleyway and onto the sidewalk and down the sidewalk to the lights and across the intersection and up the other sidewalk and into Union Station and through the various corridors and onto the train, and thirty minutes later stepped out of the train into the Departures zone of Terminal One. The roar of the jets. The scream of the jets. Why do they sound so frightening? They're just steel and rubber and alloy and fuel. They're not human. They can't hurt you.

—*I'm going to ask to take five again. I'm sorry about this.*
—*That's okay. Are you all right? You look pale.*
—*I'm fine, fine, so sorry. Just give me five.*

◆ ◆ ◆

March 8, 2022 — 22:45 GMT

—*Yes, okay, great. Sorry again about that. I've been feeling ... not well today.*
—*Late night at the pub? I won't judge.*
—*Yeah. Clams, actually.*

—Oh no. Oh, I'm sorry. I don't mind the pause. It's given me time to think.

—*About anything in particular?*

—Nothing pertinent. Not to the operation, anyway. I don't know, it's just that ... I wish I understood ... How is it that you pick the people you use? I'm nothing special. And Ivy, she, god, poor Ivy. She [inaudible]. God.

—*Are you sure there's nothing I can get you? A cigarette? Something?*

—No, no, I'm good. I'm sure you can understand, it's been a difficult. Just give me a ... [*Respondent blows nose.*] Where were we?

—*At the airport.*

—Right, right. So. Per my training. Yes. I headed immediately to Rendezvous Broadwing, the seating area just west of the Currency Exchange. Not to be confused with Rendezvous Kestrel, the seating area north of Domestic Check-Ins, or Rendezvous Peregrine, out by the taxi rank. You don't like to keep things simple, do you? If only you'd kept things simple. There were too many moving parts, if you want my opinion, and I know you don't. Your plan was clockwork; you didn't account for chaos. This isn't a criticism. But maybe if you'd minimized your points of failure, it would have worked out better for you.

—*Please, we're almost done, if you could—*

—No, you're right. I will limit my comments to the matter at hand. I digress. I've always been a digressive person, especially when under stress. Whatever remains of who I was, it can be found in the digressions.

The airport. I sat by the window at Rendezvous Broadwing, just a random seat, and waited and watched. I watched without looking like I was watching, per my training: dead eyes, focusing on the middle distance. And what was I looking for? Why, the magic trick, of course. It happened, like all good magic tricks, without my even knowing, and it came in the form of a young blond girl. She was pulling a suitcase behind her, just another spoiled college kid off to travel Europe. I'd always wanted blond hair, but instead I was gifted this luscious brown cascade — oh well. She wore a fashionable knit cap and chunky black glasses. A nerdy hipster guttersnipe. She wrestled with her luggage, then stopped, checked her phone, browsed her itinerary, whatever, her TikToks, whatever, no biggie. She wandered over, distracted, to where I was sitting, sat down next to me, still enraptured by her phone. She was there for only a second, then she was up again, on her way to check-in, and beside me on the seat was a pebbled leather duffle. I snatched it up and took off for the restrooms. I went to the middle stall for old times' sake. Inside the duffle was a boarding pass, a passport, someone else's clothes.

Wilma Blumquist.

That's who I am now, or who I'm supposed to be. Wilma Blumquist. Somehow I'll have to find a way into that name.

On the train to the airport, at the front near the driver, I'd seen Edwin from Engineering. Of all people. Edwin from Engineering. It took me a second to recognize him; I'd never seen him in civilian clothes. How many of us were involved in this? No, wait, don't answer. I don't want to know. I'm pretty sure Edwin saw me, too, but he didn't acknowledge it, of course, just kept his eyes on the floor. Toward the end of the ride he pulled his employee passcard from his pocket and dropped it between two seats. I wonder what his name is now. I wonder who he left behind. I'll stop. I'm sorry. I'm sorry.

I was sitting at Gate 16, watching TV. It was tuned to a news channel, CBC or one of those. On it, two people were talking about money. About saving for your retirement, your post-work lifestyle. Ha. And then another news guy cut in, and they switched to live footage, a helicopter buzzing around the King William Hotel. Strobing police cars surrounded the building, blue, white, blue, white. And fire trucks behind them, and three or four ambulances. The camera zoomed in. The street had been shut down, cordoned off. Something had happened; it was unclear exactly what. The police hadn't issued a statement, and the only thing the news guy knew was that a major incident had taken place late in the afternoon. I kept watching, kept waiting for it to come clear, needing to know more, leaning into the TV as if that would help me to understand, when the flight attendant came on the PA and told us to board.

—*So you felt some ambivalence about what you'd been involved in? Or something else, possibly? Concern for your co-workers? Guilt, maybe? Anger?*

—I didn't feel guilty or anything. I didn't know what to feel. Which is just as well. Although one thing that troubles — not troubles. That nags at me? The feeling. That's gone now. Of purpose. For seven years, I woke up bursting. With fear, terrible anxiety, anticipation, but also with mission. And this morning I woke up here, in my new life, and I felt. I felt vacant, hollowed out. It's the feeling when you realize that the last seven years of your life have been about just one thing. About passing a room key. It makes you feel like, what's the next thing, you know? Anyway, digressions. I get chatty when I'm anxious. The food at the hotel was decent, have I mentioned that? The fish tonight totally did not make me sick, which, you never know in certain regions. Clearly it was the right one, the decision that I made all those years ago. Although to be honest, I have to say that, don't I? No choice. I must move headlong through the tunnel. And by the way, thank you. My room here is okay, maybe not as swish as I might have hoped, but clean, seventeenth floor, all the lights of the city. Such a civilized city you have, too, so cultured. Cold tonight, I guess, for March. I didn't think it would be this cold. But you can't have everything, can you?

END OF TRANSCRIPTION
PREPARED AND SUBMITTED BY: WEBER, T.

C O N F I D E N T I A L [UNDISCLOSED LOCATION] 001411
DEPARTMENT FOR NEA/I
SUBJECT: CORRECTED COPY: ASSET DEBRIEF INTERVIEW

REF: A. [UNDISCLOSED LOCATION] 1411
Classified By: CDA Officer P. Saunders for reasons: 5.1 (a)–(c).

ASSET ID: "ENGINEERING" [Legal name Edwin Aubele]
May 29, 2022 — 14:30 GMT

83 days after Operation Fear and Trembling

—Wow, this place is great, isn't it?

—*I thought you might like it.*

—I can't believe this one escaped me. I've spent the last however long just wandering around, exploring the city. The parks, the cafés. The boulevard that everyone fishes off of. There's a museum for every interest, I swear. I don't drink anymore, but I hit a couple of bars, screw it, just to get out of the apartment. The bars here, the restaurants. The tacos, or those fermented things served on a bed of moss, it's wild. There's an urbanity I wasn't expecting. People from all over, all that human migration, and the food scene really reflects that. I've been to a few restaurants so far, but never here. This place should be on one of those Netflix food shows. So much character, wow. I love all the old photos on the walls.

—*Those are the grandparents who started the business. It's been a fixture of the neighbourhood for something like sixty years.*

—I love that. Always eat where the locals eat. This menu, holy smokes.

—*I recommend the mussels, Edwin, if you eat shellfish.*

—I'm deathly allergic, but I might make an exception just this once.

—*Just so you know, I've pressed Record, so anything we talk about will be, you know, accessible to anyone who wants to hear it.*

—I'll try not to swear.

—*Great. So this is in part a wellness check. It sounds like you've been okay? Keeping yourself busy?*

—Ish. I have my meditation practice twice a day. And I'm grateful for the phone, thank you to whomever for that. I realize it's being monitored but, fuck it, finally I can do my crosswords.

I'll maybe confess to a certain agitation, though, boredom maybe, restlessness. It's unclear to me what it is that I should be doing other than, you know, keeping myself busy. I thought you'd forgotten me out here. What's it been, two months? Since the thing, the event?

—*The operation? Almost three.*

—Well, there you go. I'm experiencing a distortion of time, an elongation and contraction. The days bleed together in isolation. Any advice in this regard, I'd appreciate it. Should I take up tai chi? Should I finally read *War and Peace*? It seems presumptuous to take on a project.

—*Okay, so first of all, I apologize for the delay. I promise we didn't forget you or your invaluable contribution, which, as I understand it, was extemporized, making it all the more impressive. But as I'm sure you can understand, given the outcome of the operation, it's been a bit of a scramble. It's been, believe me, an avalanche of paperwork. Endless reports and post hoc analysis — you know the deal.*

—I saw something about it on the *New York Times* site. It was kind of a thrill, if I'm honest, to have made it into the *New York Times*, even if it was for this clusterfuck.

Sorry, I didn't mean to —

—*It's all right. We failed to meet certain operational benchmarks, but the action overall can be designated as successful if we factor in certain other data.*

24

—Oh. Okay, well, then, great. I'm happy for … happy to hear that. Fantastic.

—*So, as well as a wellness check, this is in part an effort to establish a narrative of the day, an agreed statement of facts, if you will, that will help us to locate chokepoints and to refine our workflows going forward.*

—I understand.

—*So if you could, in as much detail as possible, recount your experience of the operation, this would be enormously helpful.*

—Sure, sure, happy to help, it's all so fresh in my mind still. Where should I …

—*Well, unless there was, you know, something unusual — I'm sure there wasn't, but maybe there was, in the week or weeks leading up to it — just start at the beginning of your day.*

—Okay, well … So I got your messages that morning, Twitter, then YouTube, then the one from OpenPuff, the postcard image, *Greetings from Copenhagen, the gardens are green.* I had had … you might call it a storm-tossed night, staring at the ceiling, 3 a.m., the bedroom blackness, the layers of shifting static, thinking about something stupid I'd said at a party to a woman in, like, 2006. Amazed at my talent to fuck up my life in ways general and specific, the decisions I've made, were they ever really decisions, or was I just, as I suspected, acting out some script written in my DNA? And now dawn had broken, here I was, cold light of day, watching all those terrible non-decisions coalesce and take their final form. Greetings from Copenhagen, the grass is green.

We have a shared dilemma, in that we are eternal spirits trapped in human shapes; we aspire to more, but we are burdened. Upon receiving your signal, I wiped the hard drive and stuffed the laptop back under my bed. Then returned to the kitchen, plucked a box of Honey Smacks from the back of the cupboard and dug around inside till I found the baggie that I'd stashed. There was less than

I remembered, but there was enough. I unzipped the baggie, laid out a rail of coke on the counter, and searched around for a —

—*I'm sorry, can we stop there for a second?*

—Sure, sure. Was I, am I rattling on? I can try to trim it back if that's more helpful.

—*No, it's just, uh … The, uh, cocaine. I'm curious, given your matter-of-fact tone, is this something you often did? Ingest cocaine before going to work?*

—Oh god, no, are you kidding? I'd have had to be in, I don't know, Management probably, to make that kind of money. No, usually I smoked crack.

—*Usually.*

—Well, regularly. Just a bit, just for a jump-start, when the thought of another day of work seemed too much to endure, an impossible cruelty. I'd been saving the coke for something special. If a record label liked my demos maybe, or a new girlfriend maybe, or the anniversary of my mom's death. But this seemed as special as anything, an end and a beginning, and also my last chance to use, because it's not like I could take it with me.

—*And so you insufflated the cocaine. And how did that make you feel?*

—Insufflated. Sure, why not? I felt great, of course. It made me feel great. The stuff was solid, my dealer knows his shit. I felt powerful. I felt like, let's get the road on the show.

—*The …*

—I mean, I could hardly wait to get doing whatever badass spy thing I was supposed to do. It's the great thing about coke. Normally I'm averse to change in all its forms, I find it traumatizing, but one line of coke and I'm a practising Buddhist: we live in a world of ephemera, yes, be fascinated, yes, take it seriously as a phenomenological matter, but don't get too attached, none of it is real in the end. It helps, this Eastern line of thought, when a big change is —

[*Respondent coughs violently, takes drink of water.*]

I'm sorry, I don't know what's wrong with me. A couple of days ago I developed this persistent dry cough. I went for a Covid test, it came back negative. It's probably just pollen. I've been going out a lot, who knows what gets into your lungs.

—*Have you been doing drugs since you've been here, or engaging in other risky behaviours?*

—No, no, no. Well ... no. I've been going to the bars, as I said, but I haven't been indulging. I just need to be around people. The coke stash in Toronto was a last hurrah. Since I've been here I've been urge-surfing, no drugs, no booze, just people. I've been getting high off of humanity, don't smirk. And everyone's been so welcoming, I have to say. I think they're curious about the foreigner. This one guy I met at a harbourfront bar took me out into the bay, predawn, to trap crab. Man, it was so peaceful. The water at that time of night smells like fish eggs, like primordial ooze. it was the darkest dark I've ever seen. We just drifted in this gently rocking crab boat, while the day spilled over the sea in a thousand purple ripples.

This other time —

— *Edwin, I'm compelled to ask, have you spoken to anyone about why you're here, your involvement with the operation, your time working for the Company? Even in passing, even obliquely? Because —*

—No, of course not, I would never do anything to, to ...

—*Because that would be a violation of the terms of your contract, as I know you're aware.*

—I would never knowingly jeopardize the Company.

—*Never knowingly. What about unknowingly?*

—No, no. If for no other reason than I'm not an idiot. I understand what a contract violation entails.

—*Do you, though?*

—Listen. I have no one. An ex-wife, I don't care what happens to her. My mom and dad are gone. My brother, well, you'd be doing him a favour. My involvement with the Company has been about me, what I need. And I like it here, in this little afterlife. I'd do nothing to fuck with it. There are palm trees here. There are toucans in the palm trees. Plus, and I mean, you can't know this, we've only just met, but I'm a grown-up. I made a deal, eyes open. I'll abide by the terms.

—*Of course. I believe you. I just had to state that for the record.*

—Sure, sure.

—*So where were we.*

—I was just going to tell you about the couple I met in the bar. I wasn't drinking, as I said. A couple of sparkling waters. They were older, this couple, friendly, looked like crabapple dolls. We got to talking. When they found out I was single they insisted I come back to their place, where they would perform some sort of ritual, cast some sort of spell. And I, in my newly discovered state of openness, thought, Well, this is fine! Why not? I'd like some companionship. I could use all the help I can get. But when we got back to their apartment, it appeared that the ritual would involve in no small part a bucket of chicken blood and a sex act with the lady, who was, I guess, a witch. And I was, well, it was all too much for me, and so it seemed best to maybe politely demur. I mean, I appreciated their concern, but, you know, I do have certain boundaries.

—*Perhaps we should get back to the day of the operation.*

—Sure, fine. Whatever you want.

—*So you snorted some cocaine, and then —*

—Went to work.

—*And how was work?*

—Same old bullshit. Fixing curtain rods, light fixtures, toilet roll dispensers. A guest has a bad moment overnight, gets some news he doesn't like from his wealth management adviser, punches a hole in the wall, why not? Some underling will fix it, he figures. People are nuts, man. I mean, deeply, pathologically fucking crazy. You learn this when you work in a hotel. The rich especially, something about the rich, the absence of existential dread, it does a number on their brains, seriously. On my morning break I called my dealer. I'd overestimated how much coke I'd stashed and underestimated how much I'd enjoy it. I got his voice mail, left a message. He's rock solid, probably he was in a meeting, he's a risk manager, works at a firm like, two blocks from the King William. An hour later, I'm working on an emergency exit door that's setting off alarms for no reason, my phone goes off, I'm excited, I pick up, "Hello?"

"Greetings from Copenhagen," a voice says.

"The gardens are green," I say.

At 2:45 p.m., the voice tells me, I am to create a distraction. A ticket will be issued to my supervisor about burned-out bulbs or some such. I am to acquire the necessary tools, exactly which ones will be left to my discretion, then proceed to the lobby chandelier, which is this immense thing in the middle of the main floor, a mountain of crystal hanging midair. When I've replaced the burnt bulbs, I am to unscrew the bottom central portion of the chandelier, and let the fucker crash to the ground. After which, the voice says, I should grab my shit and get out of there, make haste to the agreed-upon rendezvous point.

Well, this sounds great to me. Wanton destruction of hotel property? What a way to say goodbye.

I hang up. I see that my dealer has left a voice mail. This guy is on the ball, if you're ever in Toronto. At lunch, I shrugged off my coveralls, and I went to meet my dealer, in an operation at least as clandestine as your own. He was sitting at a counter in one of those food courts in the tunnels under Roy Thomson Hall, his skin spectral under the fluorescent light, immersed in whatever dumb shit was on his phone. When I sat down beside him, he stiffened, said nothing, didn't look up, just waited a minute, then stood and walked away. He hadn't touched his lunch. I reached over, un-latched his styrofoam takeout, and plucked a baggie of high-grade cocaine from his lemongrass chicken vermicelli.

—*Okay so, once again, I'd like to pause for a moment. I'm sorry, had you always had this issue? With narcotics?*

—It's not an issue. It's an attempt to solve a problem. And who knows what sort of harm might have come my way had I not had this outlet?

—*I guess what I'm saying, were you using cocaine when you were re-cruited? Did we know about this?*

—I was recruited at an NA meeting. Is this not in my file?

—*I ... Okay. I was sent a redacted file.*

—Oh yeah, well, everyone knows the redactions are where the truth lies. Yes, how long ago was that, it must be ten years. My life had melted into glass. I was a plaster cast from Pompeii, you know, frozen in perpetual cringe-mode. I'd been compelled into NA after an unfortunate early-morning incident on the Gardiner Expressway — I wasn't in a car. That's how I met Krystyna, my recruiter-slash-sponsor, in a church basement on Roncesvalles, our asses sweating into stackable plastic chairs. While the other participants spoke their truth, we locked eyes across the room and tried not to laugh. Later, at the table with the coffee and the Peek Freans, we smiled with our eyes and talked about the places we'd rather be. She wasn't like the others there. She wasn't some yoga mom who had worried her husband with her affection for a Perc and a glass of rosé. She was dark, and funny, and earthy. There have got to be better words for it than that, but you get my meaning.

I was at the beginning of a tenuous recovery, six days sober, staring with big wide cow eyes at a future without dope, what that would look like, what it would feel like, what I would do with my days, who I would become. I was vulnerable.

SEVEN DOWN

By the time you're, how old was I, forty? By the time you're forty, you've already been three or four different people. The previous Edwins I knew all about. But this new guy, this pupa with his wet, trembling wings, I had no idea who he was or what he might accomplish.

Krystyna was kind, and patient, and flirtatious. She had an asymmetrical haircut, a bigger than average nose that appealed to me. Over the next several weeks I told her, in spurts and spasms, about the previous Edwins. It's amazing how fast the meetings yoke you together, confiding your shit to a circle of strangers eating cheap cookies. Over time, Krystyna knew about my parents, about their bitching and sniping, the constant daily low-grade static, about how at some point the storm cloud they had generated broke off and took up residence in my soul. She knew about my youth — I was in a band, we played politically aware ska music and almost got a gig opening for the Specials on a reunion tour. She knew about my settled years, attempting to be married to a woman with control issues, a drab little capitalist who did not approve of my new and improved dream of becoming a recording engineer. And she knew about the thing underneath it all, the waves of inexplicable anger and sorrow that required the constant application of numbing agents.

We might have made out a couple of times, in the parking lot of the church, beside her Civic, under the weird orange light of a sodium lamp. It might have gone further than that, just one time, on a pew upstairs, after the other wastoids had cleared out. It was a skittish thing between us, noncommittal, a tenuous coming together of two people who'd been burned too many times. Or so I thought. But one day, she took it a step further. She asked if I wanted to hang out with her and a couple of her friends. I was, not excited, but open, you know, to the idea, of being the sort of person who makes new friends.

These friends, she said, were the reason she was 772 days sober. They'd given her something no other person, entity, philosophy, or practice ever had. She didn't say what that was, and I didn't press her. It sounded, I won't lie, a little culty. Red flags, you know? But I mean, here I was in twelve-step land, which is nothing if not Drunk Jonestown, so who was I to judge?

We met at a coffee shop the next Friday night. Friday night coffee shops never cease to depress me, they're like seeing an old lady in a laundromat on New Year's Eve. But this was exactly where I found myself one random Friday night, early June, ten years ago. Her friends were stylishly dressed, attractive, a couple, I assumed. Lily looked like a hipster CEO, chunky plastic glasses, power bob, perfect teeth. Dash was greying at the temples in a Cary Grant kind of way. He wore a form-fitting sweater that showcased his biceps. He took a special interest in me. Every stupid joke I made was a laugh riot to this guy. Every half-baked take on any given current event was the height of astute analysis. When he got to —

—*I'm sorry, one second. Dash and Lily?*

—Yes, why?

—*No reason, go on.*

—When he got to telling me about himself, it was like hearing my own life told back to me. An inexplicable lifelong anger, an absence of focus or direction, a bottomless sorrow that lacked an object and that could never be surmounted, but only numbed. He'd wanted so desperately to achieve something, to be good at something, be someone who was respected for his ability, but he was so easily discouraged. He flitted from one thing to the next. Everything he attempted was a failure. I couldn't believe this Übermensch in front of me had ever been a failure, but that's what he said. He echoed all the twelve-step language, too — admitting, examining, making amends, et cetera. How thick am I? It never occurred to me. That Krystyna might have … I mean, those meetings are sacred.

Dash leaned in, searching my face. "Here's my takeaway," he said, "from all those AA meetings I attended. It's maybe not what you might think. A lot of what they tell you, honestly, is just silly, new-age woo-woo, but you take what works and discard the rest. You know which of the steps really made sense to me? Step number three."

He watched me to see if I remembered. It took a moment.

"Turning over control to a higher power," I said.

He smacked his knee and grinned. "Exactly!" he said. "That was the hardest one for me to wrap my head around. I was a heathen, you know? An empiricist, I found religion unsettling. The smell of old churches? Creepy. This higher power thing, though. That's just another word for the collective. The hive mind, the matrix. When you're even just a tiny part of something larger than yourself, and you and all of the other parts are working in conjunction toward the same end, there's nothing you can't achieve."

This was Dash's pitch, for real. So either a cult or a pyramid scheme, right? But I swallowed my suspicion and, at the end of the night, gave him my phone number. A week later he met me in the lobby of an office tower at Dundas and University, the one with the Mr. Sub on the north side, and we rode the elevator to a nondescript office on the eighteenth floor, and I took a seat in a row of folding chairs, and he played me a couple of orientation videos, and I guess that's how I started with you guys. Within a couple weeks I was working at the King William, thanks to a doctored resumé and some string-pulling, I suspect, from someone you'd already planted in Management.

My first couple of years there were good enough. I learned as I went, to fix toilets and king-size bed frames and RFID locks, thanks to YouTube tutorials and a lot of trial and error. I hit my benchmarks for yearly raises, despite the perpetual outraged astonishment of my supervisor, who couldn't understand how I'd gotten the job in the first place. I kept up with my NA meetings, stayed sober, ate more legumes and leafy greens, always showed up on time. The routine was good for me, as it is for so many of us in recovery. But inevitably, after a couple of years, the tedium of the thing, the profound meaninglessness of gainful employment, the day in, day out nature of the enterprise, it wore on me. I'd been waiting and waiting for an event that never happened, you see. And so, of course, inevitably, in the absence of any kind of emotional investment, I reverted to old patterns. I'm to be commended for drawing it out, my sobriety, given the overall drabness of the situation. I contacted my old dealer, who seemed genuinely happy to see me again, although sad to see me back. Like I said, addiction is an attempt to solve a problem, and my problem was the absence of anything that didn't conspire to suffocate my soul. Outside of work I reconnected with old friends I'd wisely dropped, a sorrowful bunch of reprobates and unreliable narrators who might steal my wallet, but who wouldn't judge me, and I hooked up with old girlfriends who had done the most demeaning … who had done what they had to do to keep the dope flowing. It was a life full of dissonance. The posh hotel I spent my day in, with its spa and silver flatware, its guests with perfect teeth, its high-speed Wi-Fi and wheelchair access, its gentlemen's apparel shop and skin-care clinic, versus the hourly-rate dives I spent my nights in, with the condom dispensers in the shared bathroom down the hall, the window AC with the frayed cords, the stains on the bedding that wouldn't quite wash out. What are you writing?

—*Sorry, this is just for me. Just making a note that you were fully vetted. So great, you were at work, you met your dealer, please go on. What next.*

—Next was a plumbing issue.

—*Because of the cocaine?*

—Excuse me?

—*I'm sorry, I think I misunderstood. I assumed that maybe cocaine can give you …*

—There was a plugged toilet in one of the rooms. A guest had tried to flush a $250 Wagyu striploin steak. My supervisor felt that I was just the guy to fish it out. When I'd finished the job, I pulled out my stash and did a little bump on the bathroom counter and just stared at this steak lying in a puddle of toilet water on the checkered tile floor and I thought, Who should I call? For a, you know, just to say goodbye to. A gesture to the Edwin I was shedding. Eat the chrysalis before flying away. But after like a minute of staring blankly at the toilet steak, I realized that no one would even notice I was gone. I was the guy who, ten years from now, someone posts about on Facebook, "Hey, remember that guy Edwin from high school? Anyone know what happened to him?" I was already dead, I just hadn't realized it yet.

Midafternoon, I went out to the smokers' pit for a cigarette. I didn't know it at the time, but this would be my last Canadian smoke. It was the usual crew back there, a couple of brawny Asian dudes from Receiving; the surly bellman everyone calls Ramen; Kathy from Catering and a couple of her friends. I like Kathy, she's hilarious. She's around my age, I think, maybe a couple years older. Her hair colour is always changing — black, red. Sometimes blue, despite hotel policy. She's a little thick, in the best way. Thick with two *C*s, the kids say now. More than once I'd seen her give the finger to guests when their backs were turned, which only made me like her more. When her friends went back to work, she stayed outside and sucked back another cigarette, and then another, and then another.

"Hey, happy Monday," I said.

She didn't even look at me, just stared into the middle distance, hugging herself. She took a drag, blew a funnel cloud into the clammy March air.

"Fuck me," she said.

"You all right?" I said.

She nodded her head in a way that meant no, not yes. "Edwin?" she said. "I'm having a weird day."

"Anything you want to talk about?"

She shook her head in a way that suggested yes instead of no.

"No," she said.

She had her hair pulled back in a bun-like arrangement, per hotel policy. For the first time I noticed she had a little tattoo on her neck, behind her ear. A cat's paw.

I thought I might cheer her up. I pulled the baggie out of my pocket, cupped it in my hand to keep it out of sight of the CCTV. "Any chance I could help?" I said.

It took awhile, but she glanced over, reluctantly, it seemed to me, frowned for a second at what I was showing her, not really getting it, and I thought maybe I'd screwed up, crossed a line, done something inappropriate. But then her expression changed, her eyes went wide, a happy gasp. She looked at my face, then down at my hand, then up at my face.

"I know somewhere we can go," she said.

It was a storage unit in the sub-basement, near the kitchens. Polished cement floors, walls lined with shelves. It was like Costco in there, abounding with bulk foods: vats of olives, cisterns of mayonnaise, basins of chutney. There was a freezer in one corner. While Kathy locked the door behind us, I tipped some coke onto the top of the freezer and lined it up. I rolled up a fiver and handed it to her. "Please," I said.

"Such a gentleman," she said, and bent over and vacuumed up two lines like a pro. She ran an index finger under her nostrils. "Oh, now that is," she said, "that is … exceptional."

She handed me the straw, and I insufflated the other two lines, and we stood there, aglow, savouring the glorious burn.

"I feel like I should thank you," she said. Her eyes were large and preternaturally bright, with this dappled effect, like sunlight on a windy pond, and I remember thinking, I wonder how deep that pond goes, and thinking that was a poetic thing to think, and that I should share it with her, and so I did, but she didn't seem to hear me.

She rested a hand on her collarbone, about to maybe respond, I thought, then, in an alarmingly fast series of movements, pivoted to face me, reached out her hand, and unzipped my coveralls. I looked down at her little hand, cat scratches all over it, and looked up at those wild wet eyes.

"Yeah?" she said.

I mean, I'd always liked her, you know? She had such a sunshiney face. I could see myself waking up to that face. In a different life.

"Yeah," I said. "Sure, why not?"

So she leaned against the freezer, shimmied out of her trousers, and then pulled down her — maybe I shouldn't elaborate.

—Unless you feel there's something of significance, I think we can skip forward.

—Sure. Skip forward. I'm not sure how far. Cocaine, you know? Not one of my finer moments. So okay. We're what, post-coital, post-whatever-it-was, and maybe we did another post-whatever-it-was line, and we're sitting on the floor, our backs against the freezer. We had no reason to talk, and nothing to talk about, but talk we did, in an energized, possibly delirious way about the influence of Jamaican dub on eighties British post-punk bands, when she says, "Wait, what time is it?"

I looked at my watch, and with a jolt of horror, realized the time. I'd completely forgotten the operation. I told her it was almost 2:30.

Kathy appeared equally alarmed. She was like, "Oh fuck fuck fuck fuck fuck. I'm sorry but I have to cut this short. I have somewhere I need to be."

I was already on my feet, zipping myself into my coveralls.

She struggled with her pants, which she had in her haste pulled inside out, finally slipped them onto her legs, ran a hand over her hair, effecting no change, and told me, "You have no idea how much I needed this." Then kissed me on the cheek. "In another life," she said.

And was gone. And a moment later, I was gone, too, way behind schedule, to gear up for my final act. I sprinted up two flights of stairs and down the hall to Engineering to locate all my shit — drill and screw heads and ladder — and was just heading out the door when my supervisor said, "Whoa, whoa, whoa, what are you doing?"

My supervisor is what would happen if a can of Labatt 50 gained sentience. He had a bluish face, a boar-like demeanour, and he didn't appreciate deviations from the norm. I forget exactly what I said to him, something close to true, a light was burnt out on the lobby chandelier, I had to go fix it, and he replied, "Oh no, you don't. No one opened a ticket."

Well, this was a surprise to me. You guys said you were going to open a ticket and then you didn't. I'd attributed a superior level of competence to the Company, but it turned out the Company was as useless as I was.

So I improvised. I explained to my supervisor that I'd run into deHoog, the manager of operations, and deHoog had said to make it a priority, that given the high-profile nature of the convention, a lot of future bookings were at stake, et cetera, so we must ensure the lobby was pristine.

My supervisor did not look convinced. He had this pained grimace on his face, like a man who'd just been told his calamari dinner was really deep-fried pig anuses. "I'll look into it," he said. "In the meantime, I've got you on the ninth floor, plugged toilet."

"The Wagyu must really suck today," I said.

And I'm telling you this now in the interests of transparency, not because I screwed up in any way. I'm letting you know that there were problems, hiccups along the way, human error, absolutely, but that none of it mattered. I got there in time and did what I was instructed to do. And if my makeshift solution was not true to the last little detail, it was at least true to the spirit of the operation. I waited until he was gone and, per instructions, picked up a ladder and drill and screw heads and made my way to the lobby. Sometimes you need a ladder, sometimes you need a raft.

—*I don't think I, I don't think I quite ...*

—The story of the raft? It's a Buddhist parable, I think. You've never heard it?

—*Not that I recall.*

—It goes like this. I'm going to screw this up. A fellow on his way somewhere, back in the days of yore, finds, at the end of some dusty road, a great inland sea. He squints. Oh shit. Between him and the opposite shore is about fifty miles of choppy water.

He needs to traverse that dire expanse to get to where he's going, you see. But no bridge will stretch that far. No water taxis, there's nothing back then. So he looks around. Gathers up a bunch of old two-by-fours, car tires, et cetera. Ropes them together and fashions himself a raft. And with no small difficulty, he crosses, and once he's across thinks, Well, that worked out. Maybe I'll just strap this thing across my back in case I need it for the next great impasse.

And continues on overland. Growing ever weaker. It's hot, he's thirsty, his knees are giving out. This raft upon his back, it grinds him down for days and days until finally it comes to him. The question. Born of exhaustion. What is the purpose of this raft? And the answer in quick succession: its purpose is to float. And so, with this revelation, the man drops the raft and finds that his shoulders no longer ache, his legs no longer buckle. He is free to continue his journey.

The point being, I guess, the sea was behind him, he no longer needed a raft. What he did need now? Was a good pair of boots.

Sorry, I've been listening to a lot of podcasts. I don't have much else to do.

I met a woman here, in a café. It was, what, last week? Last week. She was standing at the bar, dressed in what looked to be a skin-tight sari made of gauze, sipping something amber. The evening's entertainment was a smiley young guitarist playing Django Reinhardt, he was honestly pretty good. But the minute I saw that woman, he and all others ceased to exist. I was helpless not to gawk at her. On a break between sets she turned around, perhaps sensing my attention. She glanced at me and I think smiled, but I'd anticipated this, and so she found me staring resolutely into my club soda, trying to play it cool. The next night I came back. And there she was again, in similarly fetching garb. She had this aggressively curly hair that was five times the size of her actual head. She was the most fantastically gorgeous human I'd laid eyes on in, well, however long it had been. This second night I was bolder. When she smiled at me during a break between sets, I morphed into Leisure Suit Larry. I nodded, I might have winked — god, how the thought of that troubles me — and I sidled up to where she was sitting.

"My name is Edwin," I said.

"Hello, Edwin," she said.

We performed the usual rituals. Chit-chat, some incidental contact, personal inquiries, and good-natured provocations designed to filter out the serial killers. She worked, she said, as an analyst for the Seven Down Corporation. I didn't ask what that was. She was single, incredibly. One child, though, he lived with his father's wealthy family. She loved hip hop, she said, and kombucha, and gardening. She showed me a mandala tattoo on her shoulder blade. Two days later we went out for dinner, this tiny crab shack, Sammy's, that only the locals know about. We talked about our childhoods, what have you, our take on things, frivolous shit, and then afterward we made out against the wall of a neighbouring surf shop. We made plans to meet the next day.

But when the next day came, we skipped the restaurant, we skipped the make-out session, and went straight to her place, a nondescript flat in a low-rise building in the south-central part of the city. It was tasteful, if a bit cold, like an Airbnb on Instagram. Framed aphorisms on the walls. *Love makes life a beautiful thing, Say yes to adventure*, that sort of thing. I thought nothing of it at the time; I was too horny. She pulled a bag of weed from a drawer of her mid-mod coffee table, dug out some rolling papers, and proceeded to roll a professional-level joint.

Yes, yes, I know. Your face — hilarious. When I said I haven't used, there was this one exception. We smoked some weed. It was floral and pungent, lovely stuff, and it produced almost immediate cerebral effects.

After the weed, we, you know, did what one does in that circumstance, alone in an apartment, I won't expand. It was just the usual, more or less, nothing of any larger significance to the Company. But afterward, I don't know, something odd happened. I mention it only because I'm hoping you might have some perspective. She drank some water from the glass on her nightstand, then got up, still naked and gleaming, walked to her closet, opened the door. "Here's where things get awkward!" she said in a singsong voice. And I in my compromised condition, with a rising disquiet that might have been either weed-induced paranoia or some legitimate fight-or-flight response, watched as she reached into her closet, dug around, and … what do you think she pulled out?

—*Not a knife.*

—Nope.

—*A rope?*

—No, neither of those. A pillow. She came back to the bed, lifted my shoulders, and tucked the pillow under my head. I tried to say something, but I could barely articulate. The weed was hitting hard, I've been couchlocked before, but this was something different. I asked her for a glass of water, but she appeared not to hear. She wandered from the bed to the bathroom, then re-emerged with a toothbrush in her mouth. I told her that something felt not right, that maybe I should call an ambulance, but she just padded back into the bathroom. I heard her spitting toothpaste into the sink. The sound of gargling, then of peeing. The toilet flushed. I told her that I was really very worried about what was happening to me, really very worried, and then I blinked, just for a second, and when I opened my eyes again the seagulls were clamouring and pink dawn light was slicing through the blinds.

She'd left a note on the kitchen counter. It took a while for her handwriting to come into focus. The note said something about marriage. *If you marry*, it said, *you will regret it, if you don't marry, you will also regret it*. Hard to argue with that. The weed had left me ravenous, I decided to raid the fridge. Inside I found a bottle of water, a stick of butter, an expired box of orange juice. I tried calling her later that day; she didn't pick up. I tried texting that night. A day later, I came back to the building and buzzed her apartment. Nothing.

And so now I feel as if something's going on, something I don't understand. I feel like I'm Anthony Bourdain in a David Lynch movie. And I was wondering if maybe you might have some insight into that.

—*Why would I have insight into anything unrelated to the Company?*

—Because maybe it wasn't unrelated. Maybe it was a whatever-you-call-it, an action, an operation. Maybe she was a spy? I don't know. I have no idea how these things work.

—*Well, if it was an operation, I personally have no knowledge of it, if that's what you're asking.*

—Mmm. That might be what I'm asking, yes. I really don't know anymore.

SEVEN DOWN

—Perhaps we should get back to …
—Yes, yes. Back to business. Where were we.
—You'd picked up your tools and were on your way to the lobby.
—Ah yes. The main event. So I snatched up my tools and made my way to the lobby to fix a light fixture that was not broken. My supervisor's bullshit interference meant that I was way behind schedule. Punctuality had been impressed upon me in my training, and I could guess what might result if I were late. I booked it through the service corridors, the ladder swinging wildly. It nearly brained a couple of my co-workers as I stumbled through corners and skidded through fire doors until, like a villain from a silent movie, bug-eyed and manic, fuelled by high-grade coke, I rolled into the lobby and beelined to the chandelier. The place was crawling with Bay Street knuckledraggers and empty-eyed goons with Bluetooth earbuds plugged into their heads. The conference that day, "Polycentric Growth Opportunities in the Global South," was some sort of agribusiness trade summit for the political-industrial nexus, with a high-end keynote speaker, so security was next-level.

I have an aversion to thuggery in all its forms — cops and toy cops, former cops for hire, secret government cops. I've had a few run-ins, given my history, so my inclination was to head the fuck out of there, but I couldn't, a thing needed to get done, so I focused as best I could on the task at hand. I set up the ladder and flipped through my toolbox. My instructions were to unbolt the column of the chandelier from the crown to a sufficient degree that the weight of the bottom dish assembly would bring it crashing to the floor, causing the kind of disruption and chaos unheard of in this town since the breakup of my marriage. Who this was meant to distract was anyone's guess, although I assumed it had something to do with the Bluetooth crew. I dug around in the pocket of my coveralls and located the remainder of my dope. I knew it was maybe not a great idea, maybe it was, in fact, a bad idea, but when have I ever had any judgment? I looked around, but of course no one was paying attention to the janitor, so. I tapped some powder onto the back of my hand and inhaled it as discreetly as I could. And then, out of my mind on adrenalin and blow, I grabbed my drill and climbed the ladder and set to work destroying the chandelier.

It felt terrific to be up there, I can't even explain, above all those human heads, like a young god. They had no idea what was to come. I would unleash hell upon them, screw their little convention, their anthropoid vanities and trifles and curiosa. I loosened the nuts on the two supporting bolts and was about to tackle the master, after which all that electric crystal would go slamming to the floor, when an old, a very old, a frail old man, a white-haired bone-rack in a yacht club blazer and ill-fitting slacks, pushed his wheelchair-bound wife — I'm assuming it was his wife and not his mistress — directly under the chandelier. I'm not even kidding. I was fucking dumbfounded. Why would he do such a thing? I want to be charitable, he seemed only half-aware of his surroundings and confounded generally by the state of the world. But for fuck's sake! I stopped what I was doing and waited. I gazed around three-sixty at all the puny humans down there, tried to recapture that godlike sensation I'd had only moments before, but then I peered down again at that frail little head directly below me, her little perm — she had a bald spot on her crown, a wad of Kleenex in her fist — and goddamn, the air just left my balloon. I waited some more. Where the fuck was he? I couldn't see him anywhere. I looked at my watch. This distraction needed to happen at 2:45 exactly. It was now 2:42 and 49 seconds. I had just over two minutes to decide whether to kill this woman or let the operation fail. I waited, I waited, and he didn't come back, and if he was anything like my dad he was probably still trying to void his bladder in the men's room. Then, with twenty seconds remaining, it came to me, that old chestnut:

perfect is the enemy of good. What the Company needed was a big generic distraction, not specifically a chandelier smashing to the ground. And so I calmed down, counted ten, nine, eight, and hoped for the best. I grabbed the top bars of the chandelier and, holding my breath, kicked the ladder out from under me. It clattered onto the marble floor and echoed through the lobby, and a murmuring crowd gathered round as I thrashed and twisted in the ether. I marvelled at my predicament. What untreated pathology had led me here, to this idiotic midair spectacle? I swung across a constellation of upturned faces, brown and black and white, their arms outstretched as if to cradle me as I fell. And fall I did, when I saw the old lady was out of danger. I waited one second, two, then let go of the light fixture and dropped through all those well-meaning cradling arms, landing on the tiles with a wet, corpse-like splat.

A moment of astral whiteness — and then peace. When I opened my eyes again I was lying on the floor. Two Bluetooth goons were kneeling over me. "You okay, bud?" I self-assessed for injury. My right ankle shot sparks up my leg and into my spine, but it was nothing another bump couldn't address. I raised my arm, and one thug took my hand and the other picked me up by my armpits. The old lady was getting attention from a number of hotel people. She seemed oblivious to the fate that had almost dropped on her head.

I thanked the thugs, said I was fine, insisted that I must report the incident to my supervisor, limped as quickly as I could to the southwest emergency exit, and went out into the leaden March air. I plucked the baggie from my pocket and did one last bump in the alleyway, my last bump ever, and took one moment to acknowledge the occasion. Then I shed my coveralls and headed, giddy and afraid, to Union Station.

And that was a wrap on my old life, my last act as a citizen of Toronto, Ontario, Canada. And also the last time I used, excepting that one time with the weed.

But that's okay, right? I must forgive myself. Recovery is a verb, not a noun, routine is important, and now, here, I have my twice-daily meditation practice, I avoid triggers, I get my steps in, I focus on the things that fill me up — my podcasts and TED Talks and sobriety newsletters — not the things that deplete me, which is pretty much everything else. I have a whole new world to explore, here in the afterlife. The only troubling thing, really, is this cough. It feels like it's getting worse. I'm sure it'll pass, as all things do, but I'm a worrier. No, scratch that: I am a person who worries. It does not define me. No other symptoms, just this weird sensation in the lungs. Maybe I'm not used to all this salty air.

Every breath is a death, they say.

—*Excuse me?*

—It's a Buddhist concept. Every breath is a birth, a death, and a rebirth, every moment. Every train we take to the airport, where does the journey begin? Where does it end? Every door we open, every door we close. It's all a rehearsal. For the thing we call death, in quotation marks, which is itself just a beginning. The important thing is, we can't hang on, there's nothing to hang on to, we must let go. And by letting go we open ourselves to new experience, new possibility. And so I let go. And open my heart to the new thing, whatever this is, and the thing after that, and the thing after that.

END OF TRANSCRIPTION
PREPARED AND SUBMITTED BY: SAUNDERS, P.

CONFIDENTIAL [UNDISCLOSED LOCATION] 005762
DEPARTMENT FOR NEA/I
SUBJECT: CORRECTED COPY: ASSET INTERVIEW

REF: A. [UNDISCLOSED LOCATION] 8921
Classified By: CDA Officer L. Petrović for reasons: 2.1 (a) and 2.2
(a)–(b).

ASSET ID: "CATERING" [Legal name Kathy Borschke]
March 7, 2022 — 19:09 EST

Day of Operation Fear and Trembling

[Preliminary comments redacted.]
—I've never been on time for anything. Seriously, my entire life. I
have no idea why this is. It's like, the most intense effort just to get
even remotely close to the appointed time or whatever. If I'm forty
minutes late, I consider myself early. My friend Shannon? Says it's
because I'm a Scorpio. She's big into organic foods, gluten-free toothpaste, you know the type. Never uses deodorant, rubs a volcanic rock
under her armpits. I love her. First Friday of every month we hold a
meeting of the Attitude Adjustment Club, which is basically just,
this is hilarious, two middle-aged chicks, messed up on weed food,
getting our dance on. Whatever. I don't care. My name's Kathy, by
the way.
—[Redacted.]
—A pleasure to meet you, [Redacted]. Enchanté. Oh man, you
wouldn't believe the day I've had. I could tell you about my day?
But you wouldn't believe it. My alarm didn't go off. That's how it
started. I'd set it to p.m. instead of a.m. So right about now, what

time is it? Around seven? Right about now it's annoying the shit out of my cat.

[*Extended pause. Respondent appears visibly distressed.*]

My cat. His name is Courtney. I named him after Love.

[*Respondent picks up purse, stands.*]

I'm sorry, can you just, excuse me a second, I …

[*Respondent leaves booth. Confirmed entry into establishment's restrooms. Returns approximately seven minutes later.*]

◆ ◆ ◆

March 7, 2022 — 19:27 EST

[*Respondent resumes seat.*]

—I'm so sorry.

—*Is there anything I can, uh …*

—No, no, thank you. I'm fine, really. I just bumped into a sad thought. I'm much better now. Where was I.

—*Um, Courtney Love.*

—Right, right.

[*Extended pause. Respondent blows nose.*]

Courtney Love, I love her, I do. Talk about attitude adjustment. In the nineties, you won't believe this, the way I'm dressed now, but I was in a band. We were good! In London, Ontario. We used to open for all the big touring acts that came through. We opened for fIREHOSE, for Radiohead when they played Centennial Hall, who else? Hole, of course, when they were at the Electric Banana. Amazing show, extremely loud. Our thing was we wore Catholic schoolgirl kilts and ripped fishnets. So original, I know. But we were good! A friend of mine from high school slept with one of the merch guys for Tears for Fears. That's a claim to fame in London, Ontario, seriously. Anyway, what I was saying:

this morning, I overslept, woke up wondering why it was light out, saw I had fifteen minutes to get to work. So that's how my day started. I splashed some water on my face, remembered to feed Courtney, sweet Courtney, then threw on my least dirty work clothes. The hotel makes you buy them, the bastards. These fugly navy pantsuits. I hope you know I would never wear something like this voluntarily. I'm more of a plaid shirt kind of gal. You have to pay me to wear this shit. Not that I'm a whore, but aren't we all whores when it comes to making rent? So I scarf a banana and head to the subway. And it's while I'm in the station, waiting for a train that isn't packed wall-to-wall with grumpy bipeds, that my day really gets weird. It's sort of hard to explain. But I work for this, this organization I would call it? It's kind of a side hustle. And there was this thing I was supposed to look out for. It's like, every day I have to check Twitter on my phone. This account I follow, they do these tweets once a morning. I know it doesn't make any sense. But anyway, I'm supposed to watch out for it, this tweet, a series of words in a row, and when I see it I'm supposed to do something for the organization. And so this morning I see it, this clue, after five maybe? Years? Of not seeing it. And of course I'm like, whoa, and I ...
—*[Inaudible.]*
—Sure, I'll have another.
—*[Inaudible.]*
—Yeah, it's a Stella.
—*[Inaudible.]*
—And you? All right, okay, he nods. He doesn't speak, he just nods. That's all right, I like them strong and silent. Okay, another round, please. And could I get, do you do nachos here? I'd like some veggie nachos, please. I used to eat meat, but I couldn't handle it anymore, the hypocrisy, factory farming, the nonstop genocide. Where was I?

—*Your morning.*

—Right. I saw you looking at her, by the way. Our server. It's okay, she's cute. And you're a young, strapping boy. Not a boy, sorry. I don't know why you're hanging out with an old broad like me, but I'll take it. Old or not, I still have talent. Just saying. Don't mind me, I'm ridiculous at the best of times, and I'm super ridiculous after I've dropped shrooms. Where was I?

—*Your morning.*

—Right, right. So now because of this agreement I have with this … organization, I'll call it, I have to rush back home and check something on the computer, which is a stupid extra step, actually there are a couple extra steps, but whatever. What do I know? I'm just an old second-generation punk with a nothing job and a gift for fellatio. Seriously, it's what I do. I'm a caterer, I cater. I provide what is desired, I comfort and amuse. Sorry, I'll stop, I'm a buffoon, I know. So anyway, whatever, now I'm super late and I have to call my kitchen supervisor, Toni, who is one righteous a-hole, and explain why I'm coming in late, and it doesn't occur to me until later — who cares? I'm not even coming in again after this. This is officially my last day of work. You can't fire me, I quit. And Toni's like, "Well, this makes for an extremely awkward situation for me. We have a breakfast banquet this morning and Emiko will have to cover for you, which is not fair to Emiko or to me." And of course I'd love at this juncture to tell her to go fuck herself, but I have to come in and deal with her, you know? Goddamn, I'm rambling. It's pent-up energy. The day I've had. I like your T-shirt. Is that a, what is that? On the front. It's like a Greek letter, except not. Modal logic, possible worlds. You'll be shocked to hear I did my undergrad in philosophy. I couldn't be bothered to finish. The most useless degree. But it kept me from gainful employment for three years, so it wasn't really all that useless, right? Anyway. Where was I?

Just kidding. I'm on the subway maybe fifteen minutes later, I can't even remember, wedged between a pissed-off-looking woman and a pissed-off-looking man, someone's coughing, it sounds like there's a wet plastic bag in her lungs, and I'm staring at these banners they place just above eye level, these advertisements, and I'm looking around and I realize they're almost all for these cheeseball community colleges. Get a better job, do a diploma with us. Change your life. You're on a subway with ten thousand other humanoids at eight in the fucking morning on a Monday, of course you want to change your life. Learn to be a video game designer. Get your degree in chinchilla ranching. Realize your dream of owning a car so you don't have to be trapped on the subway with all these other pitiful specimens. An entire industry built on exploiting your low-level desolation. How sick is that? How diseased is that?

Toni didn't acknowledge me when I finally made it in. She was standing at the prep area, back turned, but she knew it was me, you could tell. I was a mess, sweating from the mad rush to the hotel, my hair all wacky and askew. I immediately started doing stuff, like somehow this would compensate. After a while, she said, "Kathy, you're an hour and ten minutes late for work. I had to pull Emiko from the floor so she could work suites."

"I'm so sorry," I said.

"You knew we had a banquet this morning," she said.

"I'm sorry," I said.

"I don't need your sorrow," she said, "I need you to do your job. You haven't just let me down, you've let down your entire team. One more incident and I'll have to elevate this to HR."

Eat my ass, I said, you officious little power-hungry fascist.

I didn't actually say it. I wanted to say it. Some people, you know? It doesn't matter how tiny the patch of dirt, how shit-strewn the principality, they have to plant their flag. Little dictators on their little anthills. And these are just supervisors. These are just banquet captains. Imagine what they'd do if they had an army. Imagine what they'd do if they had a bureau of investigations. It's terrifying. No wonder the world is so fucked. We act like Kim Jong-Un is an isolated nutjob, but he's not, really, is he? All the hotels in the world, all the bars and banks and universities and insurance companies, they're all staffed by little Kim Jong-Uns just biding their time, waiting to be activated. Screw that, I say. I opt out. The only thing worth pursuing in life is pleasure, my friend. Epicurus was right, there's no point in a so-called higher calling. Move to Peru, teach ESL, spend your evenings smoking weed with all the other first-world dropouts.

So yeah, that's how I spent my morning, running around like a maniac, floor to kitchen, kitchen to floor, no time to think or reflect, then up to suites where I should've been in the first place.

The organization I work for, the other one, not the hotel, every month they give me a manila envelope. It has various things in it month to month, usually not much. A few stapled papers, a thumb drive, a burner. For five years, I've had no need for any of it. I just pick up the package, ignore it, hand it back next time I see Mona. She's my case manager. Today, of course, was different. Do you mind if I Juul? It's asinine, I know. I quit smoking, fuck, like years ago, and then I saw this YouTube thing on vaping and something went sproing in my head and I thought, Man, oh man, do I need me one of those. It's just nostalgic; I associate smoking with all the best times in my life, all the best sex I ever had — I was young and fit and played bass in a band. I know all these people on Facebook, friends from London. A few of them never left, a few moved back, a few will never kiss that hallowed ground again. And there's so much sentiment for that time in their lives, the punk scene in London, hanging out at the Embassy Hotel, watching bands, no cares, no need ever to accomplish anything. The past is a tentacle that's wrapped itself around their ankles. Their greatest accomplishment was some photocopied zine they made back when they were seventeen. All this angst in my newsfeed. This one chick I used to know, her status updates consist of how her kids will eat nothing but unheated Alphagetti and how she doesn't recognize herself when she looks in the mirror. I recognize her, though, she looks like herself, only old and gaunt and over-exercised. It's so strange to see your friends age. Previous generations were spared this fate; you'd graduate high school, move away, and never have to see anyone again. You could disappear. But no, not us. Now we find ourselves suddenly thrust together via the Facebook device only to realize that the cute boy with the mohawk you banged when you were sixteen has been replaced by a fifty-three-year-old Country Style franchisee with advanced rosacea. *Das unheimliche*, Freud said, the familiar made foreign. It's stranger, although less existentially terrifying, than watching yourself get old, seeing your own hair go grey, watching yourself slowly die. You'll see. It'll happen to you one day, if you're lucky.

But anyway, today. I shouldn't be telling you any of this. Today I had this thing I had to do for the organization I work for. At 1 p.m. exactly, my burner started vibrating. I was in the kitchen talking to Toni about hiccups in the service queue. "At our next team meeting," she was saying, "we need to revisit our prep-line workflow" and blah blah blah and I plucked out my phone and held up a finger and cut Toni off. "I'm so sorry," I said, pointing to the burner, "I think this is my oncologist." And rushed out to the hallway.

"Yes?" I said.

A female voice on the line. "Greetings from Copenhagen," she said.

"The grasses are green," I said.

"At two forty-five," she said, "you are to be —"

53

"Wait, wait," I said, "I can't, I'm not in a position to speak right now."

A pause.

"Ten minutes," she said.

Per my training, I was to ensure that I was in a private location so I could speak freely and not arouse suspicion. I know, sounds like a spy movie. But it's not like that. This organization, these people are super uptight. Never say anything to anyone, always be on time. They're neurotic about this stuff. They have these brutal weekend-long training sessions where they drill it into you. You tell your friends you've Airbnb'd a cottage on the piney shores of Georgian Bay, then spend two days, stone cold sober, in an office park off the 401, learning the grave importance of punctuality and secrecy. So I knew I had to be somewhere private in exactly ten minutes or there'd be, you know. Consequences. I had decided on the subway ride that probably the best place for privacy would be cold storage in the sub-basement, next to the Physical Plant offices. It's where we keep the freezers full of dead animals. The industrial-size cans of stewed tomatoes. At that time of day it would be empty.

I poked my head around the door and said, "I just have to run to the washroom for a second." And took off before I could see the look that Toni gave me. I ran down the hallway to the stair-well. The stairwell door was locked. It's never locked. I booked it down the hallway, my mind melting with the stress, toward the laundry, where there's a service elevator. It took forever to arrive. I got on, pressed L2. The doors closed. Such relief! Until I realized it was going up, not down. Up it went to mezzanine, where who of all people should embark but the Security Ghost. That's what I call her, anyway. Her real name is Rhonda. Who names their kid Rhonda? She spends her days in the Security grotto; I can only guess what it is that she does in there. As if my morning weren't bad enough. She's this weird little humanoid, positively wraithlike, frizzy black hair, pale as a line of coke. "Going down?" she said, in a way you might describe as coquettish. "Yes, Rhonda, going down," I said, and she smiled at me the way she always smiles, like she knows something. I stared at the floor and waited till she was gone, which thankfully was about sixty seconds later, when the elevator disgorged her into the lobby. "Good seeing you," she said, and flashed her little knowing smile, all gums, with these unnaturally tiny doll teeth. Fuck me, was I glad to see her go. I travelled downward. My whole life has been one big trip downward, so why stop now? The house I grew up in was this big suburban house in London, Ontario, wanting for nothing. Now I live above a weed dispensary. I made it to cold storage at 1:09, one minute to spare. I swiped my passcard and opened the door.

"Oh hey," Colin said. Colin is a junior sous chef. He was bending over a freezer, pulling little dead quails out of the mist. "Today's been a shitshow," he said, "a cocksucking dogan-faced whore of a day." I love Colin, but I could've done without him right at that very moment. "The banquet has been a disaster," he said. "Apparently multiple people were late for work or something? Ah well," he said, "who cares? Whatever makes life harder for Toni." He laughed, I laughed. The burner went off in my hand. "Shit," I said, "I have to take this." And made to leave, but he stopped me. "Let me give you some privacy," he said, "I have to go upstairs anyway."

"Hello?" I said, when he'd left. It was the same woman as before, a soft, serious voice. "Greetings from Copenhagen," she said, and I said — um, sure, another round?

—*[Inaudible.]*

—I'd like another. Another round, please. This bar, good god. This bar is absurd. I love the flocked wallpaper, nice touch. Fakey-fake ceiling, pressed tin, a dartboard nobody uses. It's like the Rovers Return. I keep expecting Ken Barlow to walk in. I don't usually come to places like this, I want you to know, but there's like nothing else remotely close. If I'm being honest, I'm vaguely embarrassed even to be here, and I have an irrational fear that someone I know might walk in and see me. I don't mean to be insulting, obviously you come here, maybe you're a regular, that's okay. I'm not a snob, really, it's just, this bar, you know? The low-cut titty tops that all the servers wear. And the crazy part is, people come here on any given Saturday night, and this is their fun thing, their little bit of debauchery after an afternoon hitting HomeSense and Sport Chek and the Golf Town discount outlet, and it makes me dream a little, wondering what their lives are like, what it is to be a normal living in a suburb off the 401. The cars they drive, the food they eat, the sex they have in their king-size Pottery Barn beds. How do they feel at night, after watching fucking Jimmy Fallon? Do they feel the roaring void open above their heads, the pointlessness of everything, the meaninglessness of existence? Do they wonder whether there's an infinitude of possible worlds but a finite amount of matter, such that their lives will keep repeating over and over in an endless number of variations, large and small? Do they think about whether the next iteration of their being will have brown eyes instead of blue? Large breasts instead of small? Whether their husband will be named Conner instead of Tanner and he'll prefer baseball over football or not exist at all, but rather be a Great Dane because in this version of existence women marry only Great Danes? Are they unnerved at this thought? At the quantum physicist's understanding of identity, which is that there is no identity as we conceive it, but only energy that combines and recombines in formulations to which identity accrues? My feet feel like they're made of talcum powder. Fuck, man, I'm flying. Which is probably why I feel comfortable telling you now that I'd like to take you to bed. Ha ha! Bet you didn't see that one coming. But I mean it. You haven't lived till you've slept with an older woman. We're warm and soft, at least I am, and we know what we're doing, and you can tell your friends that you slept with someone who slept with Courtney Love's roadie. Plus intergenerational hookups are cool, everyone's doing it. Plus you'll never have to worry about commitment. I'm one and done, son. I have a deep, deep ache, and I'd like to apply a hot compress, that's it. Then you can go back to your girlfriend, assuming you have one. I'm sure you have one. That server you've been making eyes with, I guarantee she's more work than she's worth. Look at the shine in that hair, all the foundation covering that one tiny acne scar. You'd never pry her from the bathroom mirror long enough to copulate. Unless you're quick to shoot, which, whatever, I'm fine with that, too. I realize I'm making a fool of myself, but I'm too old to care anymore. And honestly, it's the least of my worries at this moment in history. I have to pee, be right back.

[*Respondent leaves booth, taking purse. Confirmed entry into establishment's restrooms. Returns approximately seven minutes later.*]

◆ ◆ ◆

March 7, 2022 — 20:43 EST

—Anyway, Greetings from Copenhagen. I was telling you about my day. The woman on the phone. At 2:45 exactly, she tells me, I'm to be waiting by the elevators on the seventh floor. I will have in my possession a service trolley that I will discreetly procure from a source within the food prep area. I will wait until the appropriate moment, I will execute my duty, then I will flee like a terrified rabbit. She didn't say that last bit, I said that. I'm embellishing for your amusement. I want you to think I'm funny and smart. And honest, also, because of what I've just confessed to you. In the vain hope that these excellent qualities might compensate for my age and general state of dishevelment. You have gorgeous eyes, you must know that. You're so quiet. I love that, a man who listens.

[*Respondent takes drag off of vaping device, waves away vapour residue.*]

So now, for the second time in one day, I have to be somewhere on time. You can imagine the pressure, 2:45 exactly, with the service trolley. Fine, one more time I'll be on time, and then I can go back to being forty-five minutes late for everything, stumbling through doors like the Looney Tunes witch, a cyclone of hairpins and apologies. I go back to work, blah blah blah, I can't even remember what I did. My lunch was stuff I stole off the food prep counter. Colin, I mentioned him, our junior sous chef, mock-frowned at me and waggled his finger. He didn't give a shit. It was a strangely busy day today. I don't know why. Maybe the banquet, or maybe the security trolls, who seemed to be everywhere. Seriously, these guys, you've never seen such a bunch of humourless dicks. Or maybe it was just because it's Monday, and everyone spent the weekend drinking and fucking. Whatever. Some of the things I've seen, I should write a book. *King William Confidential.* I once walked into a suite, the woman had just gotten plastic surgery. Her face was swathed in bandages, there were bruises down her neck. She came to the door in her satin robe, open at the front, her boobs hanging out, her bush. She was old and saggy and sun-damaged, and she wanted me to stay and give her a massage. Umm, not bloody likely, ma'am, but if you'd like I'd be happy to call Toni for you. Another time I come in, room service, and I hear a strange sound coming from the bathroom. The guest, he's an overweight bald guy. He looks nervous, he wants me to leave. No problem, but clearly something is up. I leave, I alert Security, who tell me later they found a dozen ducklings in his bathtub. How he got them up there, no one can say. What he was planning to do with them, no one can say.

Most of the stories, though, they involve shit and dildos. Talk to Housekeeping, those are the stories you get. Shit and dildos, day after day after day. People are so weird. The little manias that gain purchase on their brain cells and fizz and multiply and swallow up their entire lives — one day they're normal functioning humans, the next they're taking a shit into a salver in a five-star hotel and putting it back onto the trolley so that some underpaid middle-aged caterer can discover it later when she's cleaning up the service. And feeling like that's normal, feeling like that's okay. And here, in this particular hotel, there's always that other dimension, too, the exercise of power. The rich believe they're rich because they are superior beings, smarter, more determined, harder working, and they love to remind you of this. Who knows, maybe they're right. My capacity to fuck around and accomplish absolutely nothing is unparalleled. It's a Gen X trait, purely demographic. You are so cute when you smile. So yeah, it was a busy day. But despite this thing I had to do for this other organization, I still had to do my own job, lest I arouse suspicion. Around a quarter to two, I couldn't take it anymore, I had to take a smoke break. While Toni was bitching out someone else, I took advantage and made for the Pit out back, near the loading docks, the place where everyone lights up. It was the usual suspects out there, a couple of guys from Receiving, and Edwin, this dude from Engineering, and of course my buddy Ramen. Ramen's a cool guy, young guy, nice looking, wavy black hair, he's a bellman, he works in Courtesy, which is ironic given that he's the least courteous guy I've ever known. He has a tattoo on his arm that says *ils mangeront les riches*, I saw it once at drinks after work. So I hang out with Ramen, he lights my cigarette, but I'm too agitated to engage, you know? Not that he's engaging with me, either, but still. We just sort of stand there, drifting out to sea on our little patches of ice, until finally he says, "No animal has more liberty than the cat; but it buries the mess it makes," which of course I recognize as a line from *For Whom the Bell Tolls*, so I reply, "The cat is the best anarchist," this little call and response, for which he gives me this big bright smile and grabs my head and kisses me on the bridge of my nose and says, "You're the only thing that made this trash job even a little bit bearable," and then he snatches up his Zippo and leaves. And like a minute later, the Engineering dude, Edwin, he sidles up to me and is like, "Check it out." And immediately I'm in alert mode thinking, Shit, is this guy going to show me his dick? So I look over, fucking obediently — the things women do to protect ourselves from violence — hoping to dispel whatever situation this is, only to find that he's holding a bag of coke in his hand. "Are you in the mood?" he says. And I'm like, "Yeah, I'm in the mood, let's go." So I take him to cold storage, where I know there will be neither people nor security cams. We do a couple lines, why not? We're not hurting anyone. Afterward he's like, "I've always really dug you, do you want to mess around?" And I'm like, fuck it, you know, he gave me his coke, nothing is for free. So we mess around a bit. No penetration, if that's what you're worried about, it was just the human connection, you know? Anyway, whatever we did or didn't do, and believe me, we didn't do anything of any importance, time passed. And at some point I realized this, and I was like, "What time is it?" And Edwin checked his watch, and it turned out it was two-fucking-thirty — I had like fifteen minutes to collect all my shit and make it to the seventh floor.

And so I gathered myself up, went straight downstairs, waited for Toni to go into the kitchen, and stole a trolley, and there's one thing I forgot to mention. There was something else I had to pick up, other than the service cart.

—*What's that?*

—A giant thing of chutney. You're shaking your head.

—*What's chutney?*

—You've never had chutney? It's like a condiment. You spoon it onto meat, commonly, and for whatever reason, I was supposed to retrieve some. So after stealing the trolley from Toni, I went straight back to the elevator and down to cold storage hoping I could be in and out, no one else would be there, no complications, time was of the essence. And opened the door — and of course, who was there but Emiko, my co-worker. She was standing at one of the shelving units, making ticks on a clipboard. She gave me a cursory look, saw it was just me, turned back to her inventory.

"Hello, Kathy," she said. Her voice was a monotone.

"Oh hey," I said, "hello, hello."

Purposefully misreading her tone, you know? She kept her back turned. She wanted me to know she was annoyed. So I used this to my advantage and made haste for the back shelves, where we keep all the condiments. It's like a little grocery store in there. Row after row of harissa and sriracha and fucking duck sauce and whole-grain mustard. I went to the farthest corner and rooted around. On the bottom shelf, at the very back by the wall, was a sealed plastic jar labelled chutney. This was weird; there was like half a wall of chutney behind me, but here was this one orphan jar, hidden away, undisturbed, like some pre-Columbian artifact. On its lid was a purple stamp that said *Copenhagen*. Danish chutney, who knew? I pulled it out. It was dusty. God knows how long it had been there, waiting for me. And how did it get there, I wonder? These people I work for, did they have someone in Receiving? Or did it go further back than that? The delivery guy? Someone in the chutney plant? I picked up the jar, something rattled around inside.

Dude, I couldn't help myself; I had to find out what it was. So I looked around to make sure Emiko was otherwise engaged, then twisted off the lid, and peered inside, and saw a large glass vial rolling across the bottom of the jar. For a brief moment I considered reaching in, opening it, but time constraints prevented further investigation. I screwed the lid back shut and put it on the trolley, and when I looked up I nearly pissed my pants because there was Emiko, standing at the end of the shelves, watching me.

She asked me what I was doing. I told her I was grabbing some chutney. "Might I ask why?" she said. I told her that Colin needed it. "You're picking up inventory for Colin now?" I mumbled something in response, I forget what. "I'm going to talk to Toni about this," she said. "This is not part of the workflow." I said that I was just doing him a favour. "That's not your job," she said. "He shouldn't be asking you to do that." I looked at my watch. I had seven minutes to get to the seventh floor.

"I think we need to have a conversation," Emiko said. "What happened this morning, showing up late when you knew there was a breakfast banquet, it was an imposition. I have my own job to do. I shouldn't have to cover for you."

"You're right," I said, desperate to get rid of her. "I'm so sorry, you're so right, why don't I meet you upstairs in, like, ten minutes, and we'll talk about it?"

The room smelled like frozen blood. All those dead quails lying in state. All the chicken breasts and tenderloins and pork bungs piled like relics in the freezers. All that trichinosis and spongiform encephalopathy. All that death. There is a structure in place, my young dude, here in the West, meant to abstract us from the reality of things. Supply chains, public relations, layer after layer of mediation. Abstract, distract, validate, and comfort. There is weird shit afoot. Lab-grown organoids, humans fused with plants, it's all out there, man, there are no restraints on the beaker-and-Bunsen-burner goons, the biotech loonies, the agrotechnology overlords. We don't even think to resist, because the thing we'd be resisting is so overwhelming and seemingly eternal. T'was ever thus, and ever thus shall be. But we don't have to take this, we can resist in our own little ways, you know? Anyway, my demeanour must have been sufficiently abject, because Emiko gave me a half-hearted smile and agreed to meet later.

"Great," I said, "ten minutes?"

And booted out of there and into the elevator and pressed the button for seven. Except that I'd only made it to mezzanine level when the elevator stopped. Of course, right? Naturally. Whenever you really need to be somewhere, right? This is my luck. The doors opened. And I found myself staring at this elderly couple. They looked lost, wide-eyed, turning to me for some sort of answer. "Miss," the man said, "we have been treated shabbily by a member of your staff." "Oh, I'm so sorry to hear that," I said, "have you talked to our general manager? He'd be the one to talk to." The man shook his head as though he were shaking off the whole idea of it. He was wearing a pink pocket square in a yacht club blazer. "She was a short lady," he said. He levelled his hand mid-chest, indicating height. "She was very rude to us." "I'm so sorry," I said, "I'm afraid I can't help you." I looked at my watch. I had two minutes to be where I needed to be. The old guy shook his head again and said, "Unacceptable. I demand," he said, "I demand that someone in this godforsaken hotel acknowledge our concerns." I just snorted. I'd had enough. "Why don't you just fuck off," I said, and hit the button that closes the doors.

"The consoling proximity of millionaires," Fitzgerald called it. You wouldn't believe the shit I've had to put up with in this job. The entitlement, the disregard. And not to go on about this, but the other day. Not the other day. Like, last month. I was watching this movie by Slavoj Žižek [*Note to office: check spelling/source DVD*], *The Pervert's Guide to Ideology*, it's called. Žižek is this pop philosopher, and this movie is mostly just him talking about one thing or another over scenes from movies. At one point he's talking about the London Riots, the other London, the one in England, about how all the British kids, down and out, had spent their lives being taught to desire things — running shoes, high-definition TVs, iPads, and PlayStations — but denied the means with which to satisfy these desires. Jobless or underemployed, on welfare. And how you can't put that kind of strain on a whole fucking class of people; something's got to give. They're going to explode. And how the riots, the arson and the looting and the smashy-smash, was not only predictable, but totally natural. They've been fed this steady diet of consumerist ideology, although they didn't actually swallow it, it swallowed them. And it felt like, you know, sitting there, watching this movie, shovelling my face full of genetically modified corn chips, that for just one moment I could think outside the things I'd been taught to think all my life, like that song by the Silver Jews, the meaning, the world. I remember the Wittgenstein: "If something has value or meaning, that value or meaning must lie outside the world." This crazy liberation, thinking outside the language in which we frame our thoughts, and it occurred to me that night that I really did have it in me. The power to resist. And it reoccurred to me this afternoon, in the elevator, as it stopped on the third floor, and then on the fourth, and then on the fifth, and then on the sixth.

My hands were white-knuckling the service cart handle. Whose effing hands were these? Awful, middle-aged hands, veiny and dry and cross-hatched with little pink claw marks, which of course was Courtney's work; he hates to be manhandled, but I always do it anyway. He's such a willful little guy. I'm an overwhelming force, but it's never stopped him from struggling.

I don't know. Maybe it was this, the thought of Courtney's struggles, that lit the fuse for my next thought: I don't have to do this. My entire life I've committed to nothing, I've never finished anything, never played a sport, never kept a guy around longer than three months, so why suddenly commit to this? Why do as I've been told like some good little girl? I didn't even know if this thing I was supposed to do, if it was a good thing or a bad thing. I was just doing it because they told me to do it, and it had required little of me until today, and it was a cool thing to roll around in my brain, like, I'm a motherfucking sleeper agent. When Toni treated me like shit, when my sister said something unkind, when some guy at a bar rolled his eyes at my proposition, it's okay, why should I care? I'm a sleeper agent and they're not. It was this fun little secret I had, a little shot of morphine to make the pain go away.

On the sixth floor, I looked at my watch. I had fifteen seconds to get there. I hit the button that closes the doors. Fourteen, thirteen, twelve, eleven, ten, nine, eight, seven ... ding ding, doors open. I pushed my service cart into the seventh floor hallway.

A moment later, not even that, the elevator next to it chimed, and the doors slid open. Inside were two people, a bellman I didn't recognize, and behind him ... my god, was it fucking really? It took me a minute to understand what I was seeing. It was! It was my buddy Ramen, the bellman with the anarchy tattoo, I swear to you, except it took a second to register this fact, so weird was the scene. It's Ramen, but he doesn't have his uniform on; he's dressed in a pinstripe suit, looking like a hedge-fund manager with per-forated earlobes. The expression on his face, I can't even describe. As if I've caught him jerking off. He's gawking at me, his eyes, my god, it's like he's trying to psychically impart something. The bellman I don't recognize reaches forward and grabs the service cart, which slips from my hands like it's buttered, and I just stand there, staring at Ramen staring at me, until the doors slide shut and they're gone. And now I'm just staring at my own reflection in the polished chrome of the doors. I look like an outpatient, my mouth hanging open like I've just seen the ghost of David Bowie. My hair has pulled from my bun; it's hovering over my head like the snakes of Medusa. My armpits are sopping, my ass crack is slick with nervous sweat. I'm telling you, I'm never on time for anything, but I made it, dude, I made it. Against all the forces of my nature, I got there on time. And I realize things didn't go as the organization planned, somewhere along the line something got screwed up, but it wasn't me.

I was thinking about this whole scene afterward, on the train to the airport. The organization, they wanted me to get on a plane and fly to some other place, and I almost did exactly that. I even got as far as the terminal. They'd warned us in training, flat out, that a failure to follow instructions would be bad for us, in ways they didn't specify. But they're not gods, and they can't hurt me if they can't find me. I should be someplace very different right now, someplace warm, I expect. Except that I happened to look down at my hands. Sitting in the Departures area of Terminal One, I looked down at my stupid old cat-scratched hands and thought, *You don't have to do this, Kathy.* I'd dropped shrooms on the express train to the airport, and it seemed they were now kicking in. The scratches on my hands squiggled and squirmed and morphed into Courtney's parting words, his final gift to me. They throbbed his message into my brain. *Discover a second face hidden behind the one you see.* That was the message he'd written on my hands. It was just like him to quote Kierkegaard. I got up and wandered around the terminal, thinking about what he might have meant. I went to the washroom. I strolled over to the place where you buy chips and magazines. Then I just kept on walking, right on out of Terminal One. I had no plan to speak of, I just knew I had to obey Courtney. Discover a second face hidden behind the one you see. I walked and walked, through all these places you're not supposed to walk, highway shoulders, the bleakest stretches of this assaultively ugly city, to a space that was once the gently swaying crops of the Mississauga nation and is now this irradiated exclusion zone, this ecstasy of free parking and conspicuous consumption, pockmarked with Costcos and craft supply supercentres and comically awful fake Irish pubs. Fifty metres to your right you can snarf down a five-dollar footlong while shopping for bidet attachments. Discover a second face hidden behind the one you see. I can't really tell you the details, but something went wrong with the thing that

SEVEN DOWN

I was involved in. And whatever it was that went wrong? I have a pretty good idea it was because someone inside that chain of events decided to resist. Someone they recruited actually believes in something, I just know it. I wish I could say it was me, but it isn't. Resistance takes certainty, and I have none. Which makes me, I daresay, an option on a cold Monday night in March. I'm ridiculous, but at least I know it, right? This fake fucking pub, what are we even doing in this place? I want to get out of here. That SUV outside, the big white one, that's yours? I was watching when you parked. It looks nice and roomy, plenty of space to stretch out. Do you want to get out of here?

You're smiling, you're not saying no. Amazing. Let's settle up. I'm buying. No, no, no, put that away, seriously, this is on me.

END OF TRANSCRIPTION
PREPARED AND SUBMITTED BY PETROVIĆ, L.

ASSET ID: "COURTESY" [Legal name Leonard Downey, aka Ramen]
December 9, 2022 — 06:35 GMT

277 days after Operation Fear and Trembling

—*Good morning, Mr. Downey. My name is [Redacted]. I'm the director of Asset Management at [Redacted]. The Board of Directors requested that I come have a chat. I understand you've expressed some concerns about your placement here at the [Redacted] facility. I would just like to assure you that —*
—It's morning?
—*Yes, 6:35 a.m.*
—Wow. [*Respondent laughs.*] What day is it?
—*Friday.*
—The 10th?
—*The 9th. Of December.*
—Friday, December 9, 6:35 a.m. Okay, wow, cool. Just slightly out of phase. I want a chair.
—*I beg your pardon?*
—I want a chair. Upon which to sit.
—*I'm sorry, you don't have a chair?*
—I invite you to study your surroundings. Do you happen to see a chair?

—How long have you been without a chair?

—What day is it again?

—Friday, December 9.

—Right. Why did I ask. I have no idea. What do I know anymore?

—I apologize, Mr. Downey. I can't imagine why you wouldn't be provided a chair. This is a lapse in Company protocol. [Redacted], bring Mr. Downey a chair immediately. Thank you. I'm afraid I've just arrived on the island, I haven't had a chance yet to orient fully. But as I was saying, I was told by your case manager that you had expressed some concerns about your placement here.

—My case manager. You mean Mona?

—Mona, sure, yes.

—So she knows? About all of this? About your "enhanced interrogation techniques"?

—I'm afraid I'm unfamiliar with that term. I'm here only to have a conversation. About the grievance that your case manager filed on your behalf. Per protocol. To allow you to air your concerns to an independent third party. I am pleased to assure you that the Company takes seriously all feedback from its contractors and will do everything in its power to see that this issue is resolved in a mutually satisfying manner.

—You're a woman.

—Is that a problem?

—What are you, number five? One, two, three, four … yeah, you're five. I can't remember my name anymore, but I can still count to five. Is this a change in tactic? What do you think you can do that the other four didn't? Some psychosexual shit? Ridicule my manhood? Number three did that already. I'm curious, genuinely. Ram a white-hot dildo up my butthole? Because that's just about the only thing they haven't done.

—The treatment that you're describing, if accurate, is ghastly, Mr. Downey, and I'm astonished to hear of it. I can't answer for my associates. As I say, I've only just landed. But I'm surprised that this has been

*your experience so far. The Company has a 95 percent positive rating
on Indeed.*
—Oh yes, I can see it in your eyes. The surprise. You are appalled
by your co-workers' behaviour. And you are very different, I can
see it, I can see it. And you will float this upstream, and your
inquiries will be taken seriously at the very highest levels of the
Company. Of course.
—*Mr. Downey.*
—Ms. [Redacted].
—*This needn't be an adversarial relationship. We can work together to
resolve the situation. Will you work with me on this?*
—Certainly, if it means I get a chair.
—*Well, that's a start. I'll take it. So as you must be aware, this conver-
sation is being filmed.*
—It is? Oh, right. The camera. Midway through the second water-
boarding, you forget the camera is there.
—*So if you could, I'm sure you've done this several times before, but
please bear with me, if you could state your name for the record.*
—Edward Snowden.
—*Please, Mr. Downey. This needn't —*
—Where's my chair?
—*A chair is on the way. If you could please state your name.*
—I'm not doing shit for you till I'm seated.
—*I assure you a chair is coming. So please, if you could, state your
name in full.*
—My name is Chelsea Manning. Now bring me a chair. And a ciga-
rette. See how I did that? The more you hold out, the more I cost.
—*This isn't a negotiation, Mr. Downey.*
—I beg to differ. This is most obviously a negotiation, and I am
most certainly in a position to negotiate. Having nothing left to
lose confers significant bargaining power. The man on his back has
all the leverage, don't you watch UFC? Combat sports?

—*It's important that you understand, whoever you were dealing with before, I'm not them. The slate has been wiped clean. I'd like to think of myself as your colleague in this, not your competitor.*

—Mmm, I can see how different you are. And I'd love to help you out, I really would.

—*Please, then. State your name. In full.*

—My name is Julian Assange.

—*Mr. Downey.*

—I want a chair and a cigarette. And some clothes. Failing that, a blanket.

—*We can't give you anything that you might use to harm yourself. Why do you need a blanket?*

—Um, you haven't noticed?

—*Noticed what?*

—That I'm naked? That it's cold in here? I mean, I'm no adult movie star, but surely you've noticed. Surely you've noticed. That I am unclothed, that I am, in fact, completely nude.

—*You look thin. Are you hungry?*

—I don't even know anymore.

—*It says here that you're vegan.*

—Well, I was, until you entered me into whatever this "program" is. Now I will happily eat your grandmother's face.

—*If we work together, if we help each other out, I believe we could get all of your material needs dealt with.*

—Uh-huh, and I help you by …

—*Simply stating your name, in full, and we can move forward in good faith, with a chair, a cigarette, a vegan meal, and some clothing.*

—My name is Leonard Donna Downey. Are you happy?

—*Great. I … I'm sorry, did you say Donna?*

—Yes, yes, I know. It's an old family name.

—*Really?*

—That's what my mom told me.

—Wow. Okay. Great. I'm going to check on the status of that chair. [Redacted], please speak to the kitchen. [Redacted], please locate Mr. Downey's clothing. Let's take a short break and reconvene in ten.

◆ ◆ ◆

TAPE SUSPENDED AT 06:52 GMT/TAPE RESUMED AT 07:07 GMT

—All right, then. The time is ... 7:07 a.m., Friday, December 9th. After an interruption of approximately fifteen minutes, we have resumed the interview with Mr. Leonard Donna Downey. My name is [Redacted]. Mr. Downey, do you agree with the summation I have provided?

—Sure.

—And do you agree that, per your request, we have provided you with a chair?

—Yes, yes. I agree that you brought me a chair, I agree that I'm sitting on it.

—Do you agree that we provided you with your clothing?

—Yes. And my clothing.

—Do you similarly agree that we have provided you with a meal of your choosing?

—I agree that you brought me something called a "meatless option" from your cafeteria, and that I choked down said option, which I would describe as some sort of false chicken cutlet on a bed of wilted arugula, and that now I feel a rising of dyspepsia in my lower abdomen.

—For my records, could you please state your name once again, and your date of birth.

—My name is Leonard Donna Downey. My date of birth is July 15, 1985.

—*Your place of birth?*
—Born and raised in St. John's, Newfoundland, Canada, North America, Western Hemisphere, Earth. You know all this.
—*And your co-workers call you Ramen.*
—Everyone calls me Ramen.
—*And why is that?*
—One time at dinner I ate a bunch of ramen. It was at this house where I lived in my early twenties, the other people there started calling me Ramen.
—*I see. And you agree that it's just you and me in the interview room?*
—Yes, I agree that there's no other person in the interview room. Fuck, dude.
—*And you're talking to me of your own volition.*
—Yes, yes, yes. I'm happy to proceed with this interrogation, I mean interview. What is it with you people?
—*I apologize, Mr. Downey. This is protocol. Do you agree that you became an independent contractor for the Company on June 29, 2010?*
—I agree that I was recruited by the Company on June whatever, 2010, yes.
—*And do you agree that on March 7, 2022, you participated in an operation organized by the Company at the King William Hotel, which at that time was your official place of employment?*
—I can confirm that I took part in an operation on the afternoon of March 7, 2022, and that I executed my duties exactly as directed and to the best of my abilities. I did not deviate in any way from executing the plan as specified by my telephone contact.
—*I should mention that sarcasm is not in your best interests, Mr. Downey.*
—Why do you think I'm being sarcastic?
—*There is a sarcastic lilt to your vocal intonations.*
—Well, if you can't read my intonations, I don't know how to help you.

—And also, you might find that an attitude of defiance is in no way productive or helpful to me in re-evaluating your placement.

—Defiant? Me? [*Respondent breaks into laughter.*] That's not in my nature.

—All right, well, if you could describe your experience of the day of the operation.

—What do you want to know? It was a day like any other, despite the weird breakfast messages you guys sent. I'm a bellman, was a bellman, was pretending to be a bellman, so I did what a bellman does. I fetched luggage like a dog, piled bags onto carts like a chimp. I smiled unctuously, grovelling for tip money. I pushed buttons, escorted guests up the escalators. I restrained myself from slapping their shitty, self-satisfied faces. I smiled and lit cigars and feigned enthusiasm about the local amenities and tourist attractions. There was a convention that day in the Windsor Ballroom — a leftist who was running for leadership of a country in the global south was pitching his country to a bunch of Bay Street vermin, energy and banking people — so the douchebag energy was amped. I swallowed the bile rising up the back of my throat and palmed their loonies and toonies. How I hated them. How I hated myself. It's all I have, this purifying hatred. At 10:30 I went out back for a smoke. At 12:30, I ate my lunch in front of the Front Office staff room. At 2:00 I had another smoke break. Somewhere in the middle of this, I took your phone call, and you told me what it was that I had to do. "At two forty-five," you said, "be standing at the elevators. A man will make himself obvious to you." So I was and he did. A man in a pinstripe suit, I don't remember his face.

"If you marry," he said, "you will regret it. If you don't marry, you will also regret it."

"Welcome to the King William," I said. He wasn't carrying any bags. I gestured him into the elevator and, before any other guests could enter, I pulled out my UTC key and put old Otis into service mode.

What I remember is his eyes. They were like … like stars, like collapsed stars, that's what his eyes were like. Superheated dwarf stars, I don't know.

We immediately began to undress. Pinstripe man took off his jacket, unnoosed his tie, dropped his trousers. I did the same. He was my height exactly, my exact build; when I stepped into his suit it fit exactly.

He nodded. I unlocked Otis and hit the button for the seventh floor, per my instructions. He turned from me to face the doors. In my memory it was an interminable trip upward, but it could really only have taken a few seconds. When the floor indicator hit 7, the doors slid open. At first there was nothing, just a generic corporate hotel hallway, but in a moment a service cart appeared, as though self-motivated, an automaton — and then, behind it, a woman.

A woman that I recognized.

It was my friend, my buddy, the only one at the hotel I gave a shit about, it was fucking Kathy. She's an older lady, works in Catering. How the hell did she get herself into this insanity? She regarded me as if I were an apparition. She looked ghastly herself, ashen and frantic and drop-jawed, her hair as tangled as a root ball, Jesus, what a sight. I was no better, I'm certain. She had a catering cart in front of her. Pinstripe man, dressed as me, grabbed the cart and pulled it into the elevator, and as the doors slid shut, the last thing I saw was her astonished eyes.

I pressed the button for the eighteenth floor. Neither of us said a word. The man's scent had permeated the suit that I now wore. It was an unsettling sensation, like I was wearing someone else's skin. When the doors opened on the eighteenth floor, pinstripe man pushed the cart into the corridor wordlessly, without looking back.

SEVEN DOWN

Per instructions, I locked the elevator and waited. I pressed my ear to the doors. I heard the cart clattering down the hallway. I heard a door open. A moment later, a fire alarm went off, I wasn't sure what to do, and then voices, shouting. This wasn't what I, no one told me to expect this. A few seconds after that, there was a volley of gunshots, impossibly loud, like popcorn exploding in my ear canals.

I panicked, I did, but I caught myself, per training, and thought through the Guidelines. It seemed to me Protocol 7.1 would apply in this situation, at least close enough. I don't know. I had to think on the fly. I don't know if I was right. Anyway, that's what I did, I aborted my involvement in the operation. I unlocked the elevator and plunged down to the main floor lobby, made my way through the mayhem, conventioneers and business assholes, oily smilers and hand shakers, out through the front door, despite protocol, because why the fuck not. My co-worker Donny, he didn't even recognize me; he opened the door and smiled joylessly and wished me a wonderful afternoon. Because now I was the pinstripe man. I walked down the front steps like a pharaoh, never to enter again. Cabbies and Ubers smiled at me, I was no longer a despicable thing; I was a dollar sign. I dug around in the pockets of my suit. I found a twenty-dollar bill, a subway token, a stick of Dentyne. Not enough for an Uber. So I popped the Dentyne and made my way to the airport.

—*And, just going through the notes now, according to my colleague [Redacted], you took the subway.*

—Yes. Why?

—*Well, it's just curious. Given your proximity to Union Station, you could have taken the airport train.*

—Dude, I spent years as a crust punk. That shit does not leave you easily. I still get the urge to Dumpster dive. The food that grocery stores throw out, man, you could feed a family.

—*Is that why you were an hour and a half late to Pearson Airport?*

—Mechanical issues on board a train.

—*Excuse me?*

—Clearly you've never taken Toronto transit. You're always an hour and a half late for everything.

—*Okay, well, we can come back to that. Right now I'm just hoping you can fill in a few holes. At 10:30, according to your own account, you went for a smoke break. Could you expand on that?*

—Okay, right. At 10:30, I went out for a smoke. And what?

—*Out back of the hotel?*

—You're supposed to go out to the designated smoking area, past Receiving. It's just a couple of picnic tables with a view of a brick wall. A little slice of Shangri-la right there in downtown T.O. Everyone calls it the Peach Pit, but no one knows why. There are a couple of picnic tables set up under an awning. We get two fifteen-minute breaks a day. Got two breaks. Got.

—*Beverly Hills 90210.*

—I beg your pardon?

—*The TV show. It was the diner where the kids hung out. The Peach Pit.*

—All right.

—*Sorry, go on.*

—I smoked two du Maurier Distinct king-size cigarettes, and ashed and butted them in a metal bucket filled with sand. Is this enough detail? I took a swig of tap water from my PVC-free bottle and went back in to kiss some more asses.

—*Mm-hmm. And were any of your co-workers out there at that time?*

—Maybe? It was nine months ago, a lot has happened since then. Yes, wait, yes, there were. A guy from I think Engineering, Edwin, he was twitchy and talkative, chewing the ear off another guy, who was from the kitchen. The kitchen guys are always out there. They like to smoke.

—*Do you recall what they were talking about?*

—Probably nonsense, knowing the parties involved.

—*And how long were you out there in the Peach Pit?*

—Fifteen minutes, give or take.

—*Are you certain? Would you like to rethink that?*

—No. What do you mean?

—*I guess I'm wondering if your memory of the smoke break might be less than optimally exact.*

—I'm telling you what you want to know.

—*According to your file here, you skipped your morning cigarette. You exited to the Peach Pit, but sat down at a picnic table for just a moment before getting up and returning to the hotel. At 10:32 a.m., we have you outside of the women's facilities on the main floor, and for the next eight minutes you're loitering next to a decorative potted palm in a manner described as "agitated." Can you confirm this?*

—Bullshit. What file? Who says they saw me? They're lying.

—*We have CCTV footage of the exterior Receiving area.*

—Let's see it, then. I was out in the Pit twice a day for how many years? And I never saw a camera. Were they ... wait. Those little domes? I thought they were speakers. If you've got footage, I want to see it.

—*I'm afraid that would be a breach of Company policy.*

—I don't care about your so-called footage, your so-called evidence, I was there, I should know. And keep in mind, okay, this was what, nine months ago? How am I supposed to remember all the tiny details of every moment of the —

And so you have this footage, and you just let me talk? For what reason? Just to, to incriminate myself?

Sure, okay, now that I think about it, maybe that wasn't the time I, maybe I didn't go out for a, maybe that was, actually, you know what? It was the day before that I saw the talkative engineer. I remember what I did now. I was intending to go out for a smoke, and worried I might run into him, and was en route to

the Pit when I came across this woman who looked almost exactly like someone I knew. From the before times, I mean, before
my servitude at the hotel. It gave me a jolt. She didn't see me,
or she pretended not to see me, she just went on walking. She
wore a hotel blazer, some sort of admin job. Different haircut,
no more mohawk, her hair was its natural colour. I couldn't be
sure it was her, but I was sure it was her. She was from one of
the other community houses, Garrison Creek Collective, over
at Harbord and Palmerston. She looked different now. Straight-
edge, clear-eyed, showered. I proceeded to the Pit and sat down,
but this sighting of Eeyore had left me rattled. So I ran back into
the building, found her, and followed her to her office. If you
have footage of me outside the women's washrooms, that's why;
her office was right beside them. It was unnerving, if I'm honest,
seeing her there. She'd been in the protest. I wondered if maybe
you'd recruited her, too.

—*I'm sorry, what was this person's name? For the file.*

—I never knew her real name.

—*By what name did you know her, then?*

—Everyone called her Eeyore.

—*And the protest you're referring to. This is the protest of the G20
summit in Toronto, Canada, in June 2010?*

—Yes.

—*Could you tell me about your involvement in the riots?*

—Protests. What do you want to know?

—*You were involved in certain incidents of note?*

—The group I belonged to took part in a legal and peaceful protest
in downtown Toronto on June 27, 2010, a date that coincided with
a meeting of the G20 nations. This should all be in your records.

—*Peaceful? This is your characterization of the event?*

—Largely peaceful, yes. The group I was involved with had no
designs or intention to cause unrest.

SEVEN DOWN

—There is some evidence to suggest that certain groups exploited the protests to advance a less noble agenda.

—Believe what you want.

—Where were you within the hierarchy of the group? A captain? Is that the right term? A foot soldier?

—Dude, there was no leadership structure. We were loose, an association of like-minded people, anarchists. There was no larger organizing principle, nothing that could in any fucking way threaten the oligarchies.

—This group, did it have a name? A guiding ethos?

—We did have a name, but that doesn't mean we were a cohesive group. Get real, dude. We were known by others as Augusta House. You're asking if we were black bloc. We were not, although this is not a claim of moral superiority. We lived together and shared theory and strategies and hosted punk shows in the basement, and on June 27, 2010, we exercised our democratic right to protest at the G20 summit, which was mostly peaceful and actually really fucking beautiful. To be part of one thought, one mind working together for one goal, all these disparate groups, Indigenous and anarchist and LGBTQ2, even the Maoists, you get it? The chanting, the chanting, the impotent cops. The feeling of transcendence, moving down Bay Street, taking it over, making it ours. It didn't belong to fucking Scotiabank anymore, it didn't belong to Ernst & Young or some cunty law firm, we were taking it back into the collective, it was no one's and everyone's. This one girl, I remember, in a black-and-white polka-dot dress, eighteen-hole Doc Martens, I smiled at her and she ran up and kissed me, with tongue, right there on the street, that's how it was that day. But then, of course, inevitably, the match was struck, the action started, and things became what they were always meant to be. Garrison Creek ran defense, barricading the riot cops, making a bunch of noise. A Montreal house, Outremont Something-Something, they ran first-string offence, boots through windows, crowbars rammed in ATMs. Augusta backed them up, we shit-bombed and spray-painted, we set off flares. The civilian protesters panicked and ran, it was chaos, pebbles of glass raining down, the screams, the orange smoke from the flares, this gorgeous violence, acrid and blooming, the squall of sirens, the aerosol stink, the skyscrapers falling down, man, international finance collapsing under the weight of its own oppression. We moved on, block by block, making the will of the people known to those who would keep us quiet, until we reached Queen Street, where the mood changed. The cops were different up there, more belligerent, and the crowd was bovine, they were amateurs. We smashed in the window of the Gap store and some hippie chicks actually booed us, if you can believe it. It was depressing, dude, the indifference, they were there just to take photos of themselves. And so it was in this atmosphere that we came across the car. Toronto Police cruiser 3367. Some cop had just left it there, in the middle of Queen Street. On purpose, it turned out. A false-flag provocation to make us look bad. Some friends from Augusta jumped up on the hood, smashed in the windows. And then a guy from Garrison Creek gave me a lighter and a rolled-up *Globe and Mail*.

—*Which you then used.*

—Yep. I'm the guy who torched the cruiser. One of the guys. One of the cruisers. *Je ne regrette rien.*

—*So whether or not you characterize yourself as black bloc, your purpose was to foment chaos.*

—No. Principled resistance. You wouldn't understand about that.

—*Then please, educate me.*

—It's called conviction. It's called bold action. It's called backing up your ideas with legitimate force. This is why your people recruited me. Or so I thought, until it sank in that all they gave me to do was to push a button in an elevator. I was capable of so much more than that, but that's what they chose for me to do. It's a fucking insult, dude.

—*All right. Well, we've gone off topic a bit. That's my fault. If we could get back to the day in question.*

—Fuck's sake. I've already gone over it. I keep going over it. For what's turning into a multitude of you people. A murder of asset managers. I don't know what you think you know, what you assume you're going to discover.

—*I'm a blank slate, Leonard. I've come into this with no assumptions. I'm just enjoying our conversation.*

—I want another cigarette. You promised me a cigarette.

—*You just had one.*

—I want a cigarette.

—*Absolutely, as soon as we fill in some —*

—First a cigarette.

—*Very well. [Redacted], let's stop the tape and come back in ten. Mr. Downey would like another cigarette.*

◆ ◆ ◆

TAPE SUSPENDED AT 08:12 GMT/TAPE RESUMED AT 08:23 GMT

—*Okay, Mr. Downey. Do you agree that you are seated comfortably?*

—Whatever.

—*Mr. Downey, I urge you to co-operate.*

—Okay, fuck. Yes, I agree that I'm seated comfortably. Yes, I agree that you provided me with a cigarette and that I smoked the cigarette and that I'm sated for the next five minutes.

—*And do you agree that it's just the two of us, that there is no one else present to coerce, intimidate, or otherwise influence your account?*

—Yes, I agree that we are the only two people in the room. Can we get on with this, please? I'm a busy man. I have to get back to my cell to jerk off. It's been so long. Since I had sex. Nine months at least, it's the longest dry spell I've had since the pandemic. Last person I touched with intent was a week before the operation. This dude I met online, I went to his place. We played video games, then got busy on his sofa. The memory sustains me to this day. He looked like that actor, who is he, played Charles Manson in a movie. And by the way, Charles Manson, did you know he was a CIA asset? The intelligence services prey upon losers and lunatics, they use them for their own ends. The Las Vegas shooter, right-wing nutjob, he was being run by an intelligence operative, that's why we still know nothing about him.

The rooms here, none of us can see each other. We speak, we have conversations, voices float out of the cinderblocks. They tell me about their wives, their girlfriends, I pleasure myself to their voices. It's amazing how our brains adjust to their context, how an empty cell can turn into a palace. But here's the situation. I like women, too, a lot, and here you are, my dude, with that little crease between your eyebrows and that businesslike ponytail, your eyebrows perfectly threaded, and that's going to be material for me for many weeks to come.

—Perhaps we could rewind. I'm not sure I have a full picture of the day. Could you start again from the beginning with as much detail as possible?

—Excellent change of subject. Okay, fine, from what point? From, okay. As much detail as possible? I woke up just after 5:30. I set my alarm for 5:30, but I always snoozed it. So ten minutes after that, I sat up, stared into the darkness. Outside, the street lights were still on, they bled through the curtains. I got up and walked to the fridge, which is about five steps from my sofa bed. I opened the fridge, pulled out some grapefruit juice and a thing of 2 percent milk. My room smelled like dust, like old people's bookshelves. I only ever noticed it first thing in the morning, the sweet, nauseating stink of it. I placed the juice and the milk on the kitchen counter, which was two steps away from the fridge. I grabbed a cup and a bowl from the dish drainer and set them on the ... Your face — hilarious. Less detail? All right. I woke up in my shitty high-rise junior bachelor, ate breakfast, picked up my phone, doomscrolled Twitter, no bullshit, all business, saw the trigger phrase from @unfavorablesemicircle, blammo. Dug out my laptop. YouTube, OpenPuff, subway, burner rings at work. What did I feel? Nothing. I suppose I felt relief. That this half life was over, this ghost life you forced upon me. Opening doors, muling luggage, like a revenant, invisible to everyone. At 10:30, I went for a smoke, no, I didn't, I saw my old friend Eeyore and followed her to her office near the women's washrooms. I did not talk to her, I simply followed, and when that was done, I went back to my elevator. At 12:30, I ate lunch in the staff lunch room. At one o'clock I went back to work, and at 2:45 I carried out my orders, after which I went straight to the station, got on the subway, and —

—*Can we stop there for a second? You say you ate lunch in the staff lunch room at 12:30, approximately. But according to your file, it appears you withdrew a large amount of money from your bank at 12:24 p.m. that very day. Two thousand dollars, according to your account. I'm wondering how you might account for this discrepancy.*

—Two thousand? Yes, shit, yes, of course I did. Thank you for pointing that out. In fact, now that I think about it, I ran down to the bank at lunch hour, withdrew some money, two thousand, as you say, and then had a quick bite in the staff room, a low-effort peanut-butter-and-relish sandwich, paired with a baggie of carrot sticks and a peach Snapple. I don't recall giving you access to my bank account.

—*I'm curious why you withdrew such a large sum of money on the day of the operation.*

—Well, it's because I didn't know what was going to happen. I thought I might need some walking-around money in my new home. If you'd given me some warning, I might have withdrawn it the day before.

—*Completely understandable. I'm sure I would have done the same in your position. And I'm certain I don't have to point out that material misrepresentation is a breach of contract. The consequences of which I know you're aware.*

—Ah yes, here it is. The threat. Couched in the blandest of corporate doublespeak. You think I'm lying.

—*I regret that you feel this way, Mr. Downey, truly. It reflects a failure on my part to communicate my empathy, and also my deep concern that you understand the implications of the contract that you have signed. If you feel in any way threatened by our conversation, I encourage you to have your case manager file a complaint. I am in no way above Company protocol. Would you like to stop this interview right now?*

—Yes.

—*Very well. [Redacted], please stop the recording, if you will. Perhaps Mr. Downey might have a better rapport with my colleague [Redacted]. Have you met him yet, Mr. Downey?*

—I don't think so. Was he one of the others ? Was he number four? Number four was an asshole.

—*No, that was [Redacted].*

—So I guess I haven't met him.

—*I think you'll find him quite businesslike. The things he's been involved in ... most of it I can't talk about, but you'd be amazed. Have you heard of* Effacer le tableau?

—Is that a movie?

—*It was a genocide. In the Democratic Republic of Congo, in the autumn of 2002. Some sixty thousand Bambuti pygmies were massacred. [Redacted] served as logistical support for the MLC. It was a train and equip mission. I should be quick to note that he was there as a contractor; he'd yet to work for the Company. Employment by the Company does not imply an endorsement of any previous or future contracts.*

—Whatever that means. Why the fuck would any right-thinking person engage in a genocide?

—*I wish I could say that he needed the money, but he didn't. He enjoys the work.*

—So this is the sort of gang you want to associate with. This junta, this *Einsatzgruppen*, this jolly band of psychopaths. You're happy to have co-workers like these?

—*Mr. Downey, I will concede to you that I dislike what goes on here at times and am doing my best to protect all of my assets, you included, from some of the less desirable outcomes.*

—Well, you sure sound like you're endorsing it. That smug, sly smile on your face. You're attractive enough, in a mainstream, cor- porate way, you're good for LinkedIn headshots, but the smugness makes you ugly.

—*Okay, Leonard, it's clear by your comments that any intervention on my part is unwelcome, so I will back off. I have no authority, mandate, or desire to represent someone who doesn't want it. And so I would recommend that you do your best to get in contact with your case man- ager, so that she might —*

—Fine, fine, fine, fine. Okay, never mind, Jesus. What is it. What is it that you want?

—*I want nothing. I'm simply doing my job. But it would make our morning infinitely less fraught if we were able to agree on a plan going forward.*

—And we do that how, how do I, what do I have to do.

—*I read your file on the flight over — case manager accounts, local media reports, your previous statements — and I will admit to some confusion. There are gaps in the record that I would very much like to*

*plug so that we can move forward with your placement and get you out
of here, into someplace —*
—Warm.
—*Of course.*
—Where should I start.
—*Just right at the very beginning again, if you wouldn't mind.*
—Uh-huh. Okay, I got to work at 7 a.m. I picked up luggage, I set
down luggage. I smiled at all the dear old one-percenters who'd de-
voted their precious lives to the meaningless accumulation of cap-
ital. I opened the doors of their limousines and ushered them inside and smiled my automated smile, the simulated smile that was
actually a shriek of desperation, and took their discreet little five-
dollar bills and thanked them for their generosity, and did this over
and over, clock ticking, time beating its drum, one step closer to
death. At one point I saw the CEO of Scotiabank, yes, I know who
he is, I consider it my business to know, and I smiled extra wide at
him, because twelve years earlier I'd shit-bombed the lobby of his
head office. Hello, sir, welcome to the King William Hotel. Splat.
I saw a famous Silicon Valley fraud, known for his unhinged tweets
and his grand plan to abandon the earth and terraform Mars. I
spied lanyards from Apple, from Huawei, from ExxonMobil and
Monsanto. There was a breakfast event that morning in the ballroom, this constant influx of plutocrats and oligarchs, lawyers and
members of Parliament, flaunting their power, apes in their finery.
I picked up luggage, I set down luggage. At 10:30 I stalked my old
friend Eeyore. Then returned to work, pushing buttons, palming
coins. At 12:20, or thereabouts, I went to lunch and ate a peanut
butter and relish sandwich and came back at one and worked the
lobby, et cetera, et cetera, until 2:37, at which point I crossed the
floor and … here's a new detail for you. I was nearly brained by a
maniac running wild with a ladder. One of the janitors; I think it
was Edwin. He'd come charging through the lobby as I made for

the elevator bank, and if he'd connected, well, there goes your little plan. Luckily it was just a glancing blow. I brushed off this near miss and stood at the lift and waited for the man in the pinstripe suit to arrive. You know what happened in the elevator. There was a problem on the eighteenth floor, as I've previously described, at which time I invoked Protocol 7.1, aborted my mission, proceeded to the subway, got on a train, then got off the train at Bathurst Station. I took the —

—*Sorry, uh, why did you exit at Bathurst Station?*

—Excuse me?

—*You said Bathurst Station. But to get to the airport you'd have to exit at … Kipling? Yes, Kipling Station.*

—I don't know. Why would I say that? I got out at Kipling. Kipling Station. From there I took the express bus to the airport, and Bob's your auntie.

—*Is this why you were an hour and a half late to the rendezvous? You got out at Bathurst Station?*

—An hour and a half went bye-bye. Who cares? I was a good little soldier. You have me on CCTV. I did what the generals told me to do. I followed my orders.

—*It's just curious, this gap between your departure from the hotel and your arrival at the airport.*

—Curious, oh yes. Your curiosity permeates your very essence. The crease between your eyes. You better watch that or it'll become permanent. Unfortunately, I can't help you. I have no idea how to … Actually, you know what? I actually can account for it, the ninety minutes. There was a delay on the train. Bathurst Station, smoke at track level. That's why I said Bathurst.

—*Was it smoke at track level? Or was it a passenger assistance alarm?*

—What?

—*I'm afraid I'm confused, because in a previous statement to my colleague [Redacted], you said there was a passenger assistance alarm.*

—No, I didn't. Anyway, what does it matter? It was either smoke at track level or a passenger assistance alarm. I mean, I've been on my feet for how many hours? They wouldn't let me sit. My brain is Jello salad right now.

—So you're saying your previous statement is the more accurate one?

—I'm not saying anything. You're just trying to confuse me. I got out at Bath— I got out at Kipling Station. There was a delay at Bathurst Station, who cares what the delay was about? Maybe it was a signal problem. Maybe it was a jumper. Have you ever been on Toronto transit?

—I'm sorry, something just caught my eye. Can we switch gears for a second? You have a sister, Janet. According to your file.

—Go fuck yourself.

—Janet, that's right, according to my file here. She's several years younger than you. Your half sister, I guess I should say. Were you close?

—You leave her out of this.

—I'm sure you're concerned about how she's doing, given her condition. Would you like an update?

—You can't touch her. You're bluffing.

—I'm just asking if you'd like to hear how she's doing. You must be desperate for news.

—There's a ton of security at the facility. You'd never get to her. Not even you and your psycho co-workers. Leave her out of this. This is between you and me. She's sick, do you understand? She's had a terrible, her life has not been good, she's ill, our mother was a drunk, we didn't get a proper start in, in, my sister is not well, she's not part of this, and for you to insinuate that, that some, that some harm might … I went to Garrison Creek. Okay? There, now you know. I went to the Garrison Creek Collective. Their house is on Harbord, corner of Harbord and Palmerston. That's why I got off at Bathurst Station. There was someone at Garrison I wanted to see, and I realized this would be my last chance to see him, and I thought what difference would it make, a few minutes late, and you promise, you promise, to leave my sister alone, yes? You promise.

—*Mr. Downey, I'm crestfallen. If I have somehow implied or suggested that your sister might come to some harm, I have misspoken and will need to choose my words far more wisely.*

—I'm giving you what you want. I'm co-operating. You leave my sister alone. I wanted to find him, the guy who gave me the newspaper and the lighter. I wanted to talk, I needed to know.

—*Know what?*

—After I'd torched the cruiser, what followed was something I'd describe as a general chaos. People shouting, scattering, giving me a wide berth, phones out, filming it all. I ran west, to Spadina, but a cordon of riot pigs pushed the crowd back. That's where the infamous kettling would happen, not long afterward. I was stuck there, cornered, just freaked out and pinned down. I didn't know where to go, I'd lost my friends, when another bloc guy, he had a Québécois accent, I assumed he was from the Montreal house, grabbed me by the elbow. "Come on," he says, "come this way." So I follow him into the Horseshoe Tavern, a woman is there in bloc gear, holding the door open. I couldn't see her face, just these huge hazel eyes under her balaclava. She pulled up the face covering so I could see her mouth, she smiled. "Comrade," she said. We exited the Horseshoe through the back door, scrambled down the alley, stripped off our gear, street clothes underneath, and hoofed it back to Augusta House. It was quiet there, no one was back yet. The only other person was Moonrat, this old guy, late forties, long greasy hair, sort of the patron saint of the house. He was on the phone, reconnoitering, finding out where people were. We collapsed onto the couches, me, the Québécois guy, and the woman with the hazel eyes. The woman asked me what the address was, she wanted to let their friends know where they were. The dude pulled out his cellphone, "*Allô, Michel? Oui ...*" Blah blah blah. I lay back, I was fried, and closed my eyes, my hand came to rest on a mound of crusty cat puke. Moonrat was playing an old Swans record on the turntable, this beauteous grinding, it made me sleepy. I think I might even have dozed off for a while, a sweet, wafting peace, long grass blowing in a warm summer breeze, no problems, no cares, until a few minutes later, a swarm of men in Kevlar vests, sidearms drawn, rushed through the front door, screaming. "Down! Down! Down!" I dropped to the floor, my cheek came to rest in more crusty cat puke. And that's how you people recruited me, seventy-two hours later, sleepless in a cinderblock room. An offer I couldn't refuse. And I try to resist wondering, though I still do, why me? When all you wanted me to do was operate an elevator. But I know what the answer is, it's why not me? You just needed a body, it could have been anyone.

So that's why I got off at Bathurst Station. I needed to find the guy from Garrison, the one who'd handed me the lighter. I needed to know if he was involved with you people, if he'd set me up. I needed to look into his eyes and see if he was lying.

—*And were you satisfied in the end?*

—Nope, didn't find him. I go there, knock knock knock, someone I don't recognize answers the door, this crust-punk girl with crucifixes tattooed under her eyes. I ask for the guy, describe him, I don't remember his name, the crust punk says she thinks she knows who I'm talking about, but he hasn't lived there in years. She invites me in, I look around, I used to go to parties there, it looks exactly the same, same curbside furniture, same ringworm couches. I half expected all my old friends to stumble down the stairs, coked up and ranting about Deleuzian theory and the films of Alain Robbe-Grillet, but they were all gone, from what she said; everyone had moved out and on. This community that had felt so eternal, it had just broken up and floated down the river. But the bloc had survived, that was the main thing. The bloc is an idea, the bloc survived even though the people had all been replaced. So there's your answer. I'm sorry I was late. I didn't think it would matter.

—*I see.*

—You don't believe me. Why don't you believe me?

—*Why do you think I don't believe you?*

—Because you're pulling on your earlobe. Was I not detailed enough? Do you want to know the colour of the crust punk's hair? It was red, the colour of fresh blood. What more do you need?

—*I'm sorry if I appear skeptical, I'm not. I'm just trying to reconcile this new information with what you've previously provided to me and my colleagues. It's all quite befuddling for someone trying to establish an organized narrative. Perhaps if we could —*

—Go over it again.

—*If you wouldn't mind.*

—Of course, I'd be delighted, but if I don't pee soon, I'll soil this lovely freshly laundered jumpsuit.

—*Very well. [Redacted], pause the recording. We'll pick up in five.*

◆ ◆ ◆

TAPE SUSPENDED AT 08:51 GMT/TAPE RESUMED AT 08:59 GMT

—*This is [Redacted], resuming my conversation with Mr. Leonard Donna Downey, after a seven-minute intermission. Mr. Downey, do you agree that it is now 8:59 a.m.?*

—Yes, I agree that the time is now whatever in the morning, though I haven't seen a clock in days and haven't slept since I last saw a clock, and what is a clock when time is folding in on itself? Anyway, I have no means to dispute this claim.

—*And do you agree that you requested and were provided with a receptacle within which to relieve yourself?*

—Yes, I agree that you let me piss into a pail before I was forced to piss all over this chair, and yes, I agree that I feel much relieved.
—And are you resuming our conversation of your own volition, without coercion?
—Yes, I agree that I'm happy to continue our rendition, I mean conversation, particularly because I have no options.
—If we could rewind to the beginning of your day, I'd like to hear once more your memory of the operation.
—From waking?
—If you might.
—Not before? You don't want to hear about my feverish dreams? Because I can still remember them. I was lying in a grassy meadow. Wafting clover, birdsong, the drone of drowsing bees. I felt something tugging at me below my waist. I looked down only to find this Che Guevara–looking dude sucking my dick. I ran my hand through his hair, he looked up and grinned, I climaxed, he burst into a thousand tiny flowers and drifted into the breeze. I jolted into consciousness after that, my brain adrip with beta waves.
—Perhaps we could focus on events relevant to the operation.
—Less detail, sure. Okay. I woke up, made breakfast, doomscrolled Twitter, watched the YouTube thing, ran it through OpenPuff, went to work, opened doors, closed doors, hauled bags, pressed buttons, took my break, came back, went to lunch, came back, executed my orders exactly as specified — I mean, it was hard, but somehow I managed to operate the elevator, years of practice, I make it look easy — heard gunshots, cut bait, got on the subway, you know the rest.
—What did you have for lunch?
—Is this a test? A sandwich, I already told you. Why? A peanut butter and relish sandwich, paired with a bag of carrot sticks and a peach Snapple.
—And you ate your lunch where?

—On a bench in a tiny wedge-shaped parkette down the block.

—*Earlier you said you'd eaten your lunch in the staff room.*

—Nope. Wedge-shaped parkette.

—*I see. You must have misremembered. It was a long time ago, as you've noted. This is likely why you've forgotten that on the day of the operation you made a purchase at 12:34 p.m. from a store called ... just a second ... Lil Punkinheads. Am I reading that right?*

—That's in your file, too.

—*It is.*

—Because, of course, you have access to my credit card.

—*Lil Punkinheads is what, a maternity shop? Is that how you'd describe it? A baby store?*

—It's a gift shop. They have all kinds of things, not just, just, not just baby shit. At the last minute, that's right, I bought a book. I wanted something for the flight, something with literary merit; those airport stores just carry junk. I went into the first place I could find.

—*Mm-hmm. What book did you buy?*

—What book? What book. *The Great Gatsby.* I hadn't read it since high school, but something was drawing me to it again. It's about a dude from the sticks who just stands around watching his buddy, this nouveau riche racketeer, try to steal away some trust-fund failson's vacant young wife. He doesn't do much, this hick, just narrates the story, doesn't intervene, no advice for his pal, he stands around watching the stupidity unfold, impotent by choice or by nature, nothing but a spectral onlooker. I'd be lying if I said it didn't have some, some, some, some resonance with my own situation. My involvement with the Company was a tour through living death, it cut me off from everything I've ever cared about. I was there still, still in the same city, but I might as well have been in the fucking Gobi Desert. The neighbourhood you moved me to, I knew no one, no one knew me. This generic high-rise in a drab, suffocating suburb out by the Don Valley Parkway. At night I'd stand on the balcony, peer down at the river of traffic, red, white, the headlights, the tail lights. All those organic lifeforms inside their machines. Where were they coming from, where were they going? A person is an entire world. For kicks I read Marxist theory, Althusser, Badiou. For fellowship, it was anonymous on-line hookups, sometimes a professional. One time, in a violation of code, I messed around with a co-worker. It only happened twice. I'd met her at a staff party, Christmas, we were mildly stoned. Sparrow, her name was, for real. This petite redhead, worked in, I think, Housekeeping. "There are things about me I could never tell you," I told her, "and you'd never believe me if I did." "Like what," she said, betraying no curiosity. There was something in her face, something so resigned, at least that's how I read it at the time. The sex was just desperate, joyless groping, but I would have continued with it if Mona hadn't somehow found out. She arranged a special off-schedule meeting by the big pond in High Park. "This will not continue," she said. It was, what month was it? Fall. The leaves were red and tenuous, they death-rattled on the branches. "You will in future refrain from assignations with your co-workers," Mona said, "do you understand? You're putting your-self at risk." She bit her bottom lip. "You endanger the operations of the Company, you risk a contract violation, and you put your-self in harm's way." She stomped off in her little houndstooth pea-coat. But she needn't have worried, because I never saw Sparrow again. Which, you know, thinking about it now, seems kind of improbable. The King Willy is a big place, for sure, hundreds of employees, but just to ghost me like that, she must have been de-termined. Regrets, I guess, a boyfriend, who knows? I didn't really care, the sex was a release, nothing more. A reminder that I was still human, full of sweat and piss and sinew. After that episode I stopped interacting with my fellow drones. You can't even guess, how lonely, how … But sometimes? Against instructions? Here's a confession. I'd sneak out of my apartment, get on the bus that took me to the other bus that took me to the subway, and down I'd go to Kensington Market. I'd walk around the side streets, Nassau, Baldwin, the cheese smell, the rotting fish, the racks of vintage denim. Then I'd stand in an alley across from Augusta House. Every Saturday there was a party, some earnest ill-starred punk band playing in the basement, I could hear them whenever someone opened the front door. I'd watch my buddies come and go, the party people in their studded leather, I'd listen to their banter while they hung out front having a smoke. Never once did they mention me. Hey, whatever happened to Ramen? Old girlfriends, old boyfriends, they were all there, but nothing. I'd been erased, I'd ceased to exist, except now as a wraith that floated up and down the elevators of the King Willy. All the things that you've done to me. The stress positions, the sleep deprivation, Nickelback on a loop. None of it compares to that punishment. Day after day, year after year, you made me lick the bootheels of the worst vermin on earth. Yes sir, absolutely sir, my pleasure ma'am, I'm sorry to hear that ma'am. There's nothing you can do to me now, you know, no essential part of me you can strip away and mutilate; you've already done it. You've broken me. Whoever I was, I no longer exist. So that's why I did that, sneak out at lunch to buy *For Whom the Bell Tolls*. I wanted to remember that, that, that feeling that, that, that … Did I say *For Whom the Bell Tolls*? I meant *The Great Gatsby*. I said *The Great Gatsby*, didn't I? I said … okay. Fuck. Okay. I want a window.

—*I beg your pardon?*

—I want a cell with a window, I want to see the sky. I want assurances in writing that you will not harm Janet. In writing. You will not harm Janet physically, mentally, or emotionally. You will let her live out her days unmolested.

—I see. Mr. Downey, it's perhaps important to note that while my colleagues and I are eager to come to a mutually satisfying resolution to this situation, my advocacy has its limits.

—And I want to be moved someplace that's warm. Wherever we are, it's cold here, and damp, and you don't heat the place properly. I want a cell with a window in a place that's warm. An island somewhere, one of your black sites. A Pacific atoll. And I want a TV. And two books of my choosing every week and, and, and cigarettes. Two, no, three packs a week, I'm not being unreasonable here.

—All right, well, feel free to jot down your requests. I can forward them to the relevant department. [Redacted], please find Mr. Downey a pad of paper and a pen. Is that all?

—And some porn. Preferably internet porn, with its panoply of subject matters, but I won't say no to DVDs.

—Okay. We'll get started on that. [Redacted]? Thank you. So, Mr. Downey, I'm a little confused. Are you telling me that this and all of your previous statements have been fabricated, either in whole or in part?

—In part.

—And your account of the day itself, is it at all factual? If you could just help me to correct our records, I'd be grateful.

—It was almost the way things happened.

—Maybe if we could go through it one more time.

—Yes, yes, yes, but I need a drink first. Just a bit of water. My throat is …

[*Respondent is provided water.*]

All right, thanks.

So. Yes. After strange, unsettling dreams, I woke up, ate breakfast, made lunch, Twitter, YouTube, OpenPuff, subway. I got to work with five minutes to spare. I picked up luggage, set luggage down. I took my break at 10:30 on the dot. Approximately one minute later, as I was heading to the Pit to have a smoke, I saw

Summer on front desk. Summer Johnson, a fellow drone, she works in Reservations. She didn't look so good.

—*So this other woman that you said you saw, Eeyore, from the Garrison Creek Collective, she was a fabrication?*

—Eeyore is a real person, but I haven't seen her in years. Last I heard she'd moved out west and become a doula. It was Summer that I saw.

She looked deeply distressed, seasick almost. It put me off my cigarette. Seriously. I went outside, sat down, and sparked a dart, but the entire ritual had been rendered joyless. So I came back in again, and as I did, caught her rushing toward a staff washroom, tearful and agitated. She didn't know this, but I was heavily invested in her well-being, and the tears concerned me. There was something going on; I needed to investigate. So I waited till she exited the shitter and returned to front desk and resumed her position.

—*Inaccurate or misleading reports are a breach of contract, the consequences of which I know you are aware. Why would you take such a huge risk?*

—Because I didn't want you to know who I really saw, and where I really was.

—*Why not?*

—Because it had nothing to do with anything. Because they're my memories, not yours. Because I wanted there to be one little piece of me you didn't own, you fucks.

I spent the remainder of my smoke break staring into the ether, and when it was time to go back I went back, opened doors, pressed buttons, hailed cabs, hauled luggage. I'm the face of the hotel, you see, the front line, an essential worker. A pansexual anarchist who once set fire to a police cruiser. Without me, the whole thing collapses. At 12:20, I broke for lunch. I snarfed a peanut butter and relish sandwich while rushing to a baby store several blocks away. When I got back to the hotel, I stuffed my new purchase into my locker and resumed my ministrations. Opening, closing, hailing, hauling.

I knew her from another life. Summer Johnson, I mean. She possessed no memory of me. We'd met at a party at Augusta House, a year, maybe more, before the G20. I was not in a good, I was in a bad, I was not well. I was out front of Augusta House, having a smoke, contemplating how I might go about doing it. Subway tracks, a stout rope, my roommate's Vicodin, a late-night swim in the lake. She came out to escape the sonic assault of whatever band had occupied the basement that night. She was high as fuck, acid, I suspect, but retained a sweet dignity nonetheless. She plonked down beside me in a garden full of dirt and weeds and empty cans of PBR, and asked me if I could see her face. I told her that I could, that it was an excellent face. She asked if I knew much about quantum mechanics. I told her I knew very little, if anything. "It's like a miracle," she said. "Science has figured out that a single particle can be in a bunch of different places at once and that two separate particles can be in conversation even if they're hundreds of miles apart. You rotate a photon in England, a different photon rotates in France. No one knows for sure why this happens. Do you know who David Bowie is?"

I told her I did.

"I heard this somewhere. That sometimes when he's writing, he'll take an old song and compose a new song on top of it. Like a pentimento, but with music. Do you know if that's true? For lyrics he'll cut up poems and news reports and other, like, ephemera, and mix them up, in parataxis, to generate weird new exchanges. And hold on, there's a point to this. Have you seen my boyfriend?"

I told her that I hadn't. As it turned out, he was in the basement bathroom hooking up with the candlemaker/polyamory activist who rented the second biggest bedroom in the house, but we didn't know that then.

"He just disappears," she said. She tilted her head and gazed, as if deep in contemplation, upon the crumbling concrete bird bath in the middle of the yard.

"I can see through space and time," she said.

Whatever my problems had been, by now I'd forgotten them completely. She reached out and snatched my hand and held it up to her face. "I'm reading you," she said. She traced an index finger along the various creases of my palm. "Your heart line is strong," she said. "You will have many lovers. But your fate line, is ... unusual." She didn't elaborate, I didn't want to know. She placed my hand back onto my thigh, gave it a squeeze, and let it go. "Don't you worry," she said. A moment later, she wobbled to a standing position and teetered back toward the house.

"I'm going to see you again someday," she said, smiling beatifically. "And we're going to have a party."

And she was gone. I sat alone in the yard a few minutes longer, vibing off her weird energy. My impulse for self-harm had completely passed. I stood up, full of wonder, and ambled home, the scent of her skin cream still on my hand.

I'd been working with her boyfriend at an organic grocery in Kensington Market. He was a super-sketchy dude, it seemed to me; he had the demeanour of a synthetic weed dealer. But he could speak with some authority about Midwest American hardcore of the eighties, so we'd talk while stocking shelves. One day, at lunch, in a burst of magnanimity, I'd invited him and his girlfriend, Summer, to an Augusta House party, why not. That was how Summer had come to be there that night. Random, random.

They broke up a few weeks after the party, and she did not fare well in the months that followed, so I heard. I kind of kept tabs on her in a half-assed manner, second-hand gossip and whatnot. The odd story drifted my way, nothing very pretty, a public breakdown, some problematic hookups with guys I sort of knew.

I stalked her on MySpace for a couple weeks. But she was never a part of Augusta House, and so months went by, then years, and she receded deeper and deeper into the past, and in time became just another thing that had happened to me.

Until, what was it, six? Seven? Eight years ago? A rainy morning, late July. I'd just started my shift. My co-worker Donny winks at me and says, "At last a good reason to come into work." He nods at the Reservations desk. And who do I see there but a bespectacled brunette with big, radiant energy, checking in a guest. It was her, Summer Johnson, the woman from Augusta House, whose loopy chit-chat saved my sorry ass one night years before. Over the course of the next few weeks at work it grew clear that she had zero memory of me — I'd offer a test smile as we passed in the hallways, and she'd respond in kind, but there was nothing in her eyes to suggest she had the slightest; she'd been too far gone that night in Kensington. Still, I kept her in my sights. I owed her something, I didn't know what, it's not like my life had been worth much, but she'd taken an interest in me, and for that she stood out. If Donny made one of his comments now, I'd smack the back of his head and tell him to shut up. At staff functions, I'd scan and hover like a Bluetooth fool, in case some dude slimed on her and forced me to intervene. At some point over the years I friended a friend of hers on Facebook and that's how I learned about Summer's newfound stability, her hard-won level of contentment, a guy named Steve. I kept an eye on Steve, as best I could from a distance. His Facebook was not locked down so he was easy to stalk. He worked at Meals on Wheels, solid job, he was a fan of the Wu-Tang Clan, *The Sopranos*, Major League Baseball. Normal person stuff. I found no fault with that. He was normal, I approved. He wasn't some walking STD who worked in an organic grocery. I was happy for her.

Although even saying this to you now, I know it wasn't really happiness that I felt, but relief that I didn't have to keep thinking about her after I was gone.

And think about her I did not, really, for some months, until the morning of the operation, when an inadvertent glance in her direction tripped the trap door that hovers always above my head, and a cascade of angst soaked me head to toe. She was on front desk with some guests. Maybe the untrained eye would never have noticed, but to me, her agitation was striking. Her movements had a darting quality to them. She dropped her pen, repeatedly. A lock of her hair had come loose from her bun, it floated gently beside her head, she hadn't noticed. I tried to put it out of my mind. I had my own shit to worry about.

At 10:30, I left for my smoke break. As I exited the lobby, I turned back to check on her. She was on the phone. She looked nauseated now, as if gripped by some violent gastrointestinal event. I was determined not to let this distract me, however, and, in fact, made it as far as the Peach Pit picnic tables when I realized I would not be able to enjoy my damn cigarette. So I turned myself around and marched back into the hotel — just in time to spot her rushing toward the staff restrooms. So that's why you saw me on the CCTV. I was following Summer.

A little later, I make a point to bump into Addilyn, a friend of Summer's, works in Reservations, too. "Oh hey," I say, as casually as I can. "Is Summer okay? I saw her in the hallway and she didn't look too good." Addilyn is failing to suppress a smile. She glances around to see who might be within earshot. Then tells me that Summer wasn't feeling well this morning. She winks. I tell her I'm not catching her meaning. Addilyn directs her gaze downward, toward her hand, which is rubbing her stomach. "You mean," I say, "she's pregnant?" Addilyn shrugs and grins. "It's exactly how I was with my first," she says, and presses an index finger to her lips. Shhh.

I was glad for Summer, I was, if that was what she really wanted. Lots of people aspire to destroy their lives with children. I respect their aspirations. I myself have destroyed my life in other ways. To each her own.

But as the morning progressed, it pressed down on me, the thought that once upon a time she had saved my life, however inadvertently, and now this new one would one day be emerging from her flesh, mewling and bloody, like the Xenomorph from *Alien*. And that I should learn the news on this of all days, the very one in which I'd be passing into my own new life. I could not have known at the time, obviously, that my new life would be at this "facility." I thought there'd be palm trees and Mai Tais. And so it felt, I don't know, imperative somehow, to mark the occasion, to finally say thank you. I know this all sounds unhinged. I don't give a shit, truly. At lunch, I withdrew the last of my money from the bank, I wouldn't be needing it. Then I hit Lil Punkinheads, bought Summer's baby a fuzzy yellow duck. And on the way to the airport, after the operation, took a little detour to her apartment. She lived on the first floor of a small red-brick building just west of Harbord and Bathurst. I got out at Bathurst Station, booted it down to her place, and stuffed the money and the duck into her mailbox. A gift from Uncle Ramen. And I hope she has a happy life and dies a shrivelled old crone surrounded by her spawn and grandspawn.

I've got you on record. I get a window, somewhere warm. A TV, some porn to keep me company while I wait.

—*Is this, excuse me. Please give me a moment. Is this, given that this is such a considerable deviation from past narratives, I'm of course curious if there are any other elements you'd like to revisit.*

—Nope, the rest of it was real. Garrison Creek is a real house, *Great Gatsby* is a real book. The sex workers, the co-worker hookup, that all happened. Eeyore was an actual person. For disinformation to really sing, you also need to tell the truth. I made up the crust punk with the crucifix tattoos, she doesn't exist. Thought she was a nice touch, though. The peanut butter and relish sandwich, although repulsive, is a real thing; my mom used to pack them in our school lunches, and I developed an affection for them.

—*Considering the numerous inconsistencies in this versus previous statements, how can I trust that your current account is accurate?*

—Well, you can't, that's your burden. And I really don't care what you believe or don't believe. I know that in the end I told you the truth, I'll take it into the ground with me, wherever you dump my remains, and you promised me a window and a TV, but no, no, you can never really know.

—*All right, I think we can leave it there for now. Unless there's anything you'd like to add.*

—I'm good.

—*Okay, [Redacted], could you please, when we're done, escort Mr. Downey back to his accommodations? I'm going to end the conversation. Mr. Downey, do you agree that this interview is being concluded at 9:45 a.m.?*

—9:45 a.m. Sure, I agree, whatever. I'll agree to anything you say. Everything is true, nothing is true, who am I to agree or disagree? And anyway, we both know how it works; whatever the truth really is, a nerd in an anonymous department, clip-on tie and pasty complexion, never sees the sun, will redact it and rewrite it, and no one will know that any of this happened, that I ever even existed, that one day a long time ago I sat in a garden on an autumn evening, street light spilling through the trees, while a pretty stranger held my hand and told me not to worry. So what even is the point?

END OF TRANSCRIPTION
PREPARED AND SUBMITTED BY: PYLYSHYN, J.

C O N F I D E N T I A L [UNDISCLOSED LOCATION] 21953
DEPARTMENT FOR NEA/I
SUBJECT: CORRECTED COPY: ASSET DEBRIEF INTERVIEW

REF: A. [UNDISCLOSED LOCATION] 6999
Classified By: CDA Officer A. al-Azmah for reasons: 5.3 (a) and (d).

**ASSET ID: "SECURITY" [Legal name Rhonda Basiago]
February 3, 2024 — 07:00 GMT**

698 days after Operation Fear and Trembling

—Thank you for meeting me. In such a beautiful spot, too. This fortification, did you know it's been here in one form or another for over four hundred years? The original structure was built in 1589. The one we see now was erected in 1763, with blocks of coquina — this is fascinating, it's a rock formed of sedimentary mollusks and whatnot, dead sea life. There's something about its internal makeup, it would confound the enemy when they assailed the fort; their rounds would be sucked into the walls and become part of the structure. I've been trying to contact you for months. [Redacted] told me when I was first placed that if I had an urgent communication, I was to text the word Kierkegaard to the number 7777, and that in the course of things I would be contacted. But I hadn't heard anything from anyone until I got your message last week.
—*[Redacted] told you that?*
—Yes.
—*Huh. Well, anyway, we're here now. Are you all right, Rhonda? You seem kind of anxious.*

—Yes, yes, I'm just, that man standing at the seawall. Does he look suspicious to you? In your professional opinion, I mean. You must be able to sense a nefarious purpose.

—*He looks like a tourist to me.*

—That mask he's wearing. Who wears masks anymore?

—*Habits can be hard to break.*

—Which is what the world government was counting on, obviously, when they unleashed the virus. We live in a time of blatant social engineering. No one even tries to hide it anymore. All the heavy metals in that vaccine, they turned us into a bunch of walking 5G receivers, primed for our latest instructions. The other side is winning. I'm worried that I might have been followed. I think someone is tracking me.

—*What makes you think that?*

—I have information about the operation, about what went wrong. About other things, too. This is why I've been trying to contact you. I wouldn't have done so if it weren't important. I need to be pulled.

—*I'm sorry? Pulled?*

—From my placement here.

—*I see.*

—They're onto me.

—*I see. Who is onto you?*

—I was hoping you might have some insight into that.

—*I'm not sure I do.*

—Well, you might after I tell you what I know. In fact, I believe I'd be more useful to you in general if I were to take a more hands-on role within the Company. I'd forgive you for thinking I've spent the last couple of years sitting on these pristine white-sand beaches drinking Mai Tais, but no, in fact, I've been working. I've been at the library, you can use their computers. I've been going down the rabbit hole, as they say. Whoever it is that's after me, whatever organization, clearly they're aware of my research and would like nothing better than to put an end to it. I'm assuming this is also why you're here? My research?

—Um, sure, although mostly this is just a standard follow-up with our retired assets.

—Because it's clear now, although I can't prove it, that they were onto me long ago, in Toronto, before the operation.

—Ah. And why do you — oh wait, by the way, where are my manners? I bought you a coffee, here.

—Thank you, that's awfully kind, but I can't. I have to be careful who to trust. I'm sure you're lovely, but we've only just met.

—Are you certain? The coffee here, it's incredible. I've only just landed, but man, oh man, I'm thinking I might stick around for a while.

—I wouldn't recommend it, personally. It's all right for a few weeks. But one begins to pine for diversion. Without which, one is … at a loss.

—So, okay, why do you suspect they, this organization, was onto you in Toronto?

—It was my neighbours downstairs. I lived on the upper floor of a two-storey building in Parkdale, on a green leafy street, with a view of a Polish church. When my neighbours moved in, that's when it all began. They were a couple. They told me their names, but I didn't bother to remember. A man and a woman. She was young-ish, thirties, he was somewhat older, mustache, greying at the sides, hair too long for my taste. An odd couple. I didn't like them from the get-go. They seemed shifty, somehow, cagey about what they did for a living. I asked them what their jobs were when we first met, they shrugged sheepishly, said they were artists, quote, un-quote. This aroused my suspicion, obviously, and also called into question the judgment of my landlord. Anyone can call herself an artist if she possesses an ironclad self-regard. "What kind of art," I asked them. They exchanged glances. "Performative body art," one of them said, I forget which. I let the subject drop, I didn't want to know. The noise and the smells started up soon after. The disorder. At first I thought it was the by-product of a chaotic lifestyle, a TV on too loud, too late, a penchant for sandalwood incense, if that's what that smell was, which aggravated my allergies, the unrecyclable things they dumped in the recycling bin. Of course I let them know, of course they apologized, or pretended to, at any rate. But after a time, weeks, months, it began to feel deliberate, these insults to my personal space. I'm sorry, would you mind if we walked? That man with the mask, he's distracting me.

—*Sure, no problem.*

—Thank you. I can't imagine why he's just … lingering. Anyway, my neighbours. The man who lived there before, he'd been so quiet, so eerily quiet, but now suddenly, with these two oily characters, there were dusky tête-à-têtes on the front stoop, and cannabis smoke; I'd slam my windows shut almost every night. There was laughter through the floorboards at odd hours, when you wouldn't expect someone to be laughing. There were lime-green thongs coiled up on the laundry-folding table. But most persistently, there was a strange phenomenon, or so I thought at first, as I drifted off to sleep, 9 p.m. on weeknights: a soft, nebulous sound, insistent, it would push its way into my pre-sleep. And I would rouse reluctantly to hear it more clearly, a bleating, a pleading, it would push up through the floor and occupy my dreams, and for the next half hour I'd be hostage to their sex. I'd wake up, pound on the floor, but they wouldn't care, maybe they didn't hear me over their moaning, maybe they'd forgotten that someone was sleeping on her side, a pillow between her legs, ten feet above their heads. I'd listen until they finished — always with a guttural braying, a tortured donkey's cries, followed by a beautiful moment of nothing — then I'd hug my pillow and stare at the empty spot beside me, and almost doze off again, except that the moment of nothing was, without fail, followed by their cacophonous snores. Excuse me for a moment, I have to Purell. I always Purell when I'm stressed, it calms me down.

—*So what exactly made you believe that your neighbours were tracking you?*

—I can't say for sure, but that's no surprise, that's part of it, that's how they operate, they're the shadows in the cracks. They knew I knew, that's all I know. Certain postings online. I'm well-regarded in the Reddit community, particularly the subreddit r/conspiracy. My username is ilovebabyotters, I have more than fifteen thousand posts, and almost as many followers. Whoever is behind my harassment has surely taken note.

—*Did you make any attempt to resolve the issue with your neighbours?*

—Of course, but the attempt was strictly performative; I knew there'd be no resolution. It's important always to put your complaints in writing, so that's what I did, I typed up a detailed list of their infractions, with dates and times, and taped it to their front door so that they couldn't claim to have missed it, then I sent an email to the landlord. An hour later I get a knock on the door. It's the woman, she's brandishing the letter in her fist. "What the heck!" she says, only she doesn't say heck, she uses a much coarser word. "What the heck is wrong with you, Rhonda?" she says. "We're under your surveillance day and night? Are you hecking crazy?"

Well, I'm not crazy. It's the world that's crazy, I'm just one of the ones who can see it. It's about seeing the pattern that's hiding in the tiny specks of light, just connect the dots and now you have Orion, now you have the Big Dipper. Most of us, sadly, accept world events, be they historical or geopolitical, as they're put forward by various interested factions, lamestream media, or other organs of propaganda, but look closer, through the pretty picture, at the one they've painted over, look at Picasso's guitarist; that pretty blue paint is hiding a woman's face. Bits of wide-body airliner wash up on a beach in Mozambique, we are meant to believe they belong to Malaysian Airlines Flight 370. The corporate media will tell you MH370 went missing one evening after diverting its flight from Kuala Lumpur to Beijing. Sure, the flight path was diverted, sure, a bunch of so-called wreckage bobbed up months later. But the unfortunate reality is that MH370 diverted not into the Andaman Sea, as was originally reported, but rather followed in the contrails of another Boeing 777 flying into Kazakhstan, landing at the Baikonur Cosmodrome, in all likelihood, in a Russian-backed operation the purpose of which one can only speculate. So you see, it's one thing to have an *A* here and a *Z* there, but it's quite another thing to fill in the crossword.

—Mmm. What kind of tree is that?

—Excuse me?

—The big one with the spiky leaves. I'm sorry, a bit off-topic, but it's just so striking, isn't it?

—I have no idea. It's not really my area. I've been focusing on other things.

—It looks prehistoric, the bark.

—I guess so, I haven't paid much attention.

—So, okay, sorry, refresh my memory? What was your role in the operation?

—You don't know?

—So yes, obviously I know, but if you could just reiterate what your actual role was within the hotel, and within the operation specifically, that would be totally helpful, for purposes of this interview.

—Sure. Security, Loss Prevention, whatever you want to call it. We're on mezzanine level, near Management. We have access to, not everything, not the suites, not certain other areas, not restrooms obviously, but most other places within the facility. Guest Comfort, my unit, is a windowless room, no distractions, banks of monitors pulling feeds from all over the hotel. I watch the movement of humans, the trails of light they leave in their wake. They're all just fireflies. The day of the operation, there were two of us on the feeds, myself and Mohammed. This was uncommon, usually there were three of us, including my manager — Travis, that awful man, I'll tell you about him later — but it was an unusual day as you know, all kinds of third-party security, contractors, all kinds of muddle. Our job that day was just to step back, keep an eye on things, stay out of everyone's way.

It wasn't until approximately 10:35 a.m. that I noticed a pattern of movement among hotel staff. It was subtle at first, hard to catch, but the more you're on the feeds, the more you develop a feel for what's right and wrong, and I began to sense that the rhythm of the day had been somehow disrupted. I could see certain staff appearing in places where they had no business being. A hotel is a machine, there's an ebb and flow; it runs according to certain predictable sequences.

Feed 3, for example. The Feed 3 camera takes in the southwest main floor corridor — offices, mostly. Edwin, from Engineering, happened to be there. This in itself was not unusual; there's no determining where Edwin or any of the other engineers will be on any given day. He had his tools spread out in front of him; he was working on the emergency exit, a malfunctioning alarm. Why, you might ask, was I even on Feed 3? What compelled me there? I've asked that question myself. An intuition? Some unknowable hand pulling the strings? Edwin is a talented musician, exotically handsome, he uploads his music to Bandcamp, you can listen online for free. It's a mix of traditional Argentinian music with various electronic bleeps and blurps, but it's quite beautiful, all the same. It's melancholy. He's had a hard life, partly by design, I suspect, not that I've spent a lot of time thinking about … Anyway, what do I know? You extrapolate from a few crumbs of someone's internet detritus. A person is a world. A few hours after this, I would see

Edwin on Feed 1A swinging from a chandelier, as if he were F. Scott Fitzgerald or something, a diamond as big as the Ritz. But right then, on Feed 3, something … slightly off-key, I guess you would say, happened. He was cranking away on the door jamb, doing his thing, when suddenly he went rigid, and dropped his wrench. He dug around in the pocket of his coveralls, pulled out a phone. He stood. Paced back and forth, up and down the corridor, talking to someone on the phone. There's no sound on the feeds. I tried to read his lips. He hung up, I analyzed his expression, he expressed nothing. For thirty seconds he stood staring at the opposite wall. Then he looked up, straight into the camera, straight at me. I felt myself jerk back, as though he could see me through the monitor, there at my desk, watching him. He held my gaze for several seconds, no expression on his face, until finally, my god, finally he smiled, he tugged at the lapels of his coveralls as though to make himself look presentable, then he waved at me. And here's an odd thing, I waved right back. Can you imagine? Me in my room, on the other side of the screen. I don't know what possessed me. A little wavy-wave, like I was a little girl with a lollipop.

I suppose I'm not used to it, people noticing me. Even when I'm right there in the same room, they seem oblivious to me. So strange, on the street, in the hallways of the hotel, people would knock into me, they'd look startled, then they'd offer a grudging apology, like they half suspected that I'd played some nasty trick on them. On the subway, waiting for the doors to open, men, women, complete strangers, would stand not an inch in front of me, intruding on my personal space, as if we were lovers, as if we were Argentines about to do the tango. I'm nothing, I'm spectral, a human-shaped patch of mist. And the same is true in my professional life: just a spectre, my hard work goes unrecognized, I work double shifts and no one seems to notice, I patch the camera feeds, update the software, I anticipate threats that no one else seems to care about, and never a raise, never a job-level increase. More than a few times they forgot even to pay me. How does something like that happen? I thought it was automated. My employee number vanished from their accounts, so they claimed. That's why I was worried, you see, my messages to Central ... I'd been told this placement would be temporary, but it's been almost two years with no communication. I thought you'd plunked me out here and forgotten I even existed.

—*I'm sorry about that. We've been a tad snowed under, to be honest. The Company is in a bit of a transition right now, there have been distractions. But you were saying. The day's rhythm had been disrupted.*

—Mm-hmm, yes. It was a few hours later, on Feed 9, not long before the operation started, that I noted another aberration, this time outside the convention floor women's facilities, just to the northeast of the Imperial Room. A tiny black-haired woman was loitering around outside. It was Ivy from Systems. Ivy is one of our more crisp and disciplined employees, few personal quirks, very professional. The only betrayal of a different, more fanciful side is her taste for elaborate manicures. Normally I would have known it was her right away, but the context threw me. I'd never seen her on that floor. The Systems office is on mezzanine level, just down the hallway from Security. Ivy maintains a fairly consistent routine day to day, she rarely deviates. She's unremarkable in that sense, she keeps her head down, her yearly performance appraisals are uniformly positive. Her personal life I'm not so sure about. I'm not one to judge other people's lifestyle choices, but sometimes you just have to scratch your head. A few years ago, at a staff Christmas party, I happened to catch her husband on Feed 2 openly gawking at Summer Johnson's decolletage. Summer is admittedly a sweet little thing, but this to me was a wildly inappropriate thing to do in the presence of your spouse. I zoomed in closer to see if Ivy had noticed and reacted. Sure enough, Ivy was right there beside him, watching him watch her, an inscrutable smile on her face. Perhaps they're polyamorous, who knows, not my business. But as I say, something there does not quite align with how she presents herself at work. Anyway, day of the operation, I'm watching her on Feed 9, she's outside the women's restrooms. Hovering, is how I would describe it, for several minutes. Then quickly makes her way inside, and then, just as quickly, exits. She keeps her head lowered, as though by lowering her head she'll keep herself from being noticed. I can't read her expression, but her comportment betrays her: at one point she appears to falter, she reaches out, braces herself against a potted palm. Her body, I could be taking some poetic licence here, but her body seems to convulse, as if she's in some distress. In a moment she collects herself and rushes out of frame. I'm sorry, that man behind us, is that the same one who was at the fortification?

—*No idea. Maybe? Wasn't the other one wearing a red mask, though? I can't remember.*

—He might have changed his mask. I think it's the same guy. You see? This is what they do, they make you doubt your own eyes. Same exact thing happened in Toronto with my neighbours and their break-ins. They did their best, but never once did I think I was losing my marbles.

—*I'm sorry, break-ins?*

—Mm-hmm. It was after I wrote the complaint letter that the break-ins began and my neighbours revealed the true purpose of their tenancy. It was subtle at first, I only half noticed it when I came home from work: a coffee mug I left on the counter moving, as if of its own volition, to the kitchen table. A pen that I distinctly remembered setting down beside my mouse pad transporting itself several centimetres to the left. One evening I found the loofah on the edge of the bathtub — who leaves a loofah there? Never in my life. The milk carton in the fridge now suddenly sitting to the left of the guava juice instead of the right, as if I'd ever do that. And I could go on.

Over time it dawned on me what was happening. They were nosing around, my neighbours, attempting to find out what they could, although to what end I'm still unclear. Perhaps they wanted to compromise my position within the Company, to flush me out, expose me. Or perhaps their interest had been piqued by my on-line postings, perhaps I was getting too close to exposing their various not-so-secret activities. Which of course, if that were the case, would mean that they were Illuminati, the Bilderberg Group possibly, about whom I'd written extensively, or the World Economic Forum, or someone employed by them. The net effect of their little intrusions was insidious, whether they intended it or not. They were subtle enough that initially, anyway, I began to wonder if I was losing my purchase on reality, to question everything I knew to be true. This is of course by design; our confusion is their nourishment. I set up cameras, obviously, one at the front door, another in the kitchen, and others in the bathroom, the living room, and the bedroom. But they must have had some ability to disable them remotely, because my daily reviews revealed nothing of note. Again, this is Illuminati 101, everything in the shadows, leave no trace behind; the very absence of evidence is the evidence. I put up with I don't know how many more weeks of travelling TV remotes and subtly disturbed underwear drawers until finally, as they were bound to do, these people crossed a line.

From time to time over the last several years, while I've been working for the Company, I've found myself in need of the services of a professional. If you understand my meaning. Mona is aware of this, she helped me to arrange it, this should all be in my file. When the loneliness became too much to bear, I needed some pampering, if you will. Generally I resisted these urges as long as I could, but always finally I would ... break down. Well, anyway, one evening I. Found myself at one of these junctures and I. Made the phone call. There was nothing dirty involved, it wasn't like that. The woman would come over and just cradle me in her lap, press me against her bosom, tell me that I was a good girl, that she loved me. And I know what you're thinking, but it wasn't some adult-baby kink, it was much more complex than that, so please keep your judgments to yourself. The point of me telling you this is that the next day, my downstairs neighbour, the woman, passing me on the front walk, stopped and said, "I didn't know you had a daughter."

"Pardon me?" I said.

"Your visitor last night. I saw her go in. I just assumed."

The look on her face. Her eyes twinkling. That malicious, knowing smile.

It was then that I decided enough was enough, I wasn't going to live like this anymore. So I called Toronto Police, not because I thought they were any match for these two people or their employers, but because at least now there was a chance that my neighbours' activities would be entered into some sort of official database and potentially trigger an Interpol investigation. I was listening at the window when the two cops knocked at their door. I couldn't make out much, one of the cops said something about a complaint, something about a domestic disturbance, which is what I had called in, and then the woman neighbour said, "What the eff, are you effing serious?" And yelling up toward my apartment, "Rhonda, get the eff down here and explain to us what the eff it is you think you're doing!" A demand that I ignored.

Thinking about it now, I don't know. I might have made a strategic error by phoning the police. Because only a few days after this incident, the sonic attacks started.

—*This is all very interesting. Sonic attacks.*

—The effects of which I'm still feeling to this day.

—Okay, we can talk about that later, but I'm going to suggest maybe we get back to the day of the operation, I think that's the information that could be of the most use to us.

—Anything I can do, I'm here to help.

—Um, so maybe if you could give us a detailed account of your instructions and how you carried them out.

—My first contact was at home, during my morning routine. I received the signal from @unfavorablesemicircle and ran the YouTube video through OpenPuff. Which, I'm sorry, if I might indulge myself for a moment? I loved that part of it, the steganography, an image hidden within another image. I admit I'm a bit of a nerd, this kind of thing thrills me. Whoever thought to employ that kind of cryptography, I applaud them. And who knows, maybe I'll get to meet them someday. I assume you have a cryptography unit?

—I have no idea.

—Okay, well.

—Probably we do. I'm new.

—Okay, well, anyway. After I got the decrypted message, *Greetings from Copenhagen, the gardens are verdant,* I opened the package for March. The package for March included a clear plastic polybag full of a yellowish powder. I tucked the polybag into the side pocket of my purse and brought it to work, as indicated by Protocol 3a(b) of the Guidelines. I was mystified at first, I'll admit this, about what it could possibly be for, but at 10:30 a.m. it all came clear. I was on my break when I received the call from my contact on the Company-issued mobile. My phone contact now advised me what to do with it. "At two p.m. precisely," she said, "you are to empty the contents of the polybag into your co-worker's beverage. If your co-worker doesn't have a beverage, you will procure one for him." He didn't, so I did. "Hey, Mo, I'm running down to the vending machine, is there anything you want? My treat!" I bought him a black coffee, two sugars plus the powder. After this I wait. Ten minutes go by, I glance at Mohammed. He's sitting in front of his monitors, sweat trickling down the back of his neck, his collar is damp. I wait. Five more minutes, I'm startled from my work by an obscene belch. In a moment, Mohammed gets up and sprints from the room. The contents of the polybag, my phone contact had assured me, were a nonlethal substance that would cause nothing more than intense gastrointestinal distress. "Your co-worker will be indisposed for several hours," she'd said, "but will be perfectly normal within three days to a week." What's three days to a week of intestinal distress? It's a blip. I lock the door behind Mohammed, I sit back down. "Disable all primary alert systems," my phone contact had said, "emergency exits, elevator overrides." I do as told, it's accomplished in a matter of minutes, I simply log in to the MM8000, all done. The hotel is now completely vulnerable, a dog with its belly exposed. When that is done, she'd said, back up all camera feeds from the MM8000 into the supplied external drive. This takes a little more doing, but I remember my training, I channel my stress into the task at hand, and in the end all feeds are captured for the period my contact had specified, from 2:30 to 3:30 p.m. I checked them myself before securing the drive in a Company-issued valise. Have you had a chance to view them?

—*Oh yes. They've been passed around, believe me.*

—Wonderful. I'm so glad. Yes, it took a bit of doing, as I mentioned before, but it's gratifying to hear that my work has been acknowledged by the higher levels of the Company. I watched all the feeds, everything, as best I could, as it came in. And felt considerable anxiety for the duration of that time. We really should have had cameras in the restrooms, it would have been nice to keep an eye on Mohammed's progress. Not that I wanted to watch him vomit and retch and whatever else, I'm not some internet creep, but the last thing I needed at that moment was a knock on the door, that fizz of fear, Mohammed wanting back in. At any rate, this was an oversight in hotel security coverage, not in your plan. I browsed the monitors, the goings and comings. There are cameras in the alleyways, adjacent to the elevators, near all of the exits.

It was just after 2:45 that I began to see the operation unfold. On Feed 10b, which draws from the overhead camera in the second of the north bank elevators, I watched a guest enter, followed by a bellman. The bellman I knew, everyone calls him Ramen, I'm not sure what his real name is. The guest I don't remember much about, he was nondescript, medium height, medium build. I recall that he wore a pinstripe suit. What drew my attention was the contravention of norms: bellmen don't accompany guests unless they're just checking in. But Ramen carried no luggage. He inserted his elevator key to switch the cab to service mode. They exchanged no looks, no casual chit-chat. And then, as if by some unspoken agreement, the two men began tugging at their belt buckles and shrugging off their jackets. I will confess to some awkward feelings here, I was uncertain what I was about to witness. They hung their shirts from the handrail, they stepped out of their trousers, kicked off their shoes. When they'd stripped down to their underpants, each picked up the other's clothes and put them on, as though they were playing dress-up. They knotted their ties and smoothed out their sleeves, then Ramen unlocked the elevator and set it into motion. At the seventh floor, Ramen stopped the elevator once more.

I switched to Feed 7. And to my astonishment, who did I see there but Kathy, from Catering. She was standing in the hallway by the elevators, clutching the handle of a service cart. I love Kathy, she's one of my favourites, she brings a certain energy and irreverence to the feeds. More than once I've caught her giving the middle finger to her supervisor when she has her back turned, or flipping off one of the guests. It's harmless, no one's the wiser, and it lends some variety to my days. But it was a surprise to see her there on the seventh floor, it caught me off guard. In a bit of a state, too, she appeared to be panting, out of breath, and her hair was more of a mess than usual. She swiped a sleeve across her forehead. When the elevator doors opened, she startled — and stood there a moment, staring, saucer-eyed, agape, at the scene inside the elevator cab. Clearly she wasn't expecting to see Ramen. They're friends, but what does she really know about him? It's astounding, the secrets we keep. As it grew plain that Kathy wasn't budging, the guest now dressed as a bellman stepped from the elevator, slipped the cart out from under Kathy's hands, and pulled it into the elevator. The doors closed.

When the elevator was gone, Kathy continued to stand there, immobile, for a minute, maybe more. Then, at length, plucked what looked to me to be a marijuana cigarette from behind her ear, and a lighter from the pocket of her tunic, and then lit up, in grievous violation of hotel policy, not that I was in a position to do anything about it.

Back to Feed 10b.

Ramen restarted the elevator, and at a floor I now know to be the eighteenth, the top floor, the Royal Suites, the elevator stopped, and the guest, now bellman, exited, pushing the service cart ahead of him. When he was gone, Ramen hit the Close Door button, and once the doors were shut, collapsed against the rear wall.

Now here's something not everyone knows. The Close Door button doesn't actually do anything. Manufacturers install it to serve as a kind of pressure release valve, so that we don't act out in their elevators. It offers us an illusion of control.

Anyway, Ramen. He was sitting on his haunches, rubbing his eyes with the heels of his palms, collecting himself, I suppose, until, mere moments later, a fire alarm sounded and he bolted upright, stepped to the door, and pressed his ear against it, listening.

SEVEN DOWN

I switched to Feed 18, the eighteenth floor corridor, in time to see two humongous bodyguards, unknown to me, rush from the makeshift security suite, through the onslaught of the overhead sprinklers, to room 1801, where Carlos Linera was staying. I knew little about Mr. Linera at the time, he was just the keynote speaker at the day's conference. We know all about him now, though, don't we? Everyone in the world knows him now. The beloved activist leader, champion of the common man, who stood up to big tech, big pharma, big oil, and the kleptocracies that enabled them, such a lovely little fairy tale.

Several seconds later, I was — was I surprised? I was interested. To see Mr. deHoog, the hotel's GM, following them. I never would have dreamed he'd be a part of this. He's a supercilious kind of person, or so I'd thought, too self-involved to participate in any project larger than himself. Forever adjusting his hair or his tie in any mirror or reflective surface that he happens upon. He followed at a remove, slug-like. Reluctant, it seemed to me, to see what kind of trouble he was heading toward, he stepped softly down the corridor. With a slight pan of the camera, the bodyguards came back into view. They were standing at the threshold of Suite 1801, arms outstretched, aiming their sidearms, Glocks or SIG Sauers, I couldn't be certain. They were shouting into the room. One of them pressed a finger onto the Bluetooth in his ear, said something into his lapel mic. Mr. deHoog inched forward, dragging his hand along the wallpaper as if to slow himself. Eventually he came up behind the others at the door and, as he did, flinched, they all flinched, bright flares of light on the monitor, and they doubled over as if from a punch to the gut. Three big bursts of mist broke from their backs. The feeds are low resolution, they're black and white, it's difficult at times to understand what you're seeing, but here it was obvious, as one, two, three sprays of pixelated viscera shot across the corridor, and they fell backward onto the carpet.

The bodyguards appeared to have discharged their weapons before going down, and now from their supine positions, one of them squeezed off another few errant rounds before succumbing to his injuries. I leaned into the screen, as if somehow proximity might give me more information. All three lay motionless in a pile on the floor. I tried to detect the rising and falling of their chests. It was unclear to me what the proper course of action was. Attempt to call back my phone contact? Send a tweet to @unfavorablesemi-circle? I knew that, according to Protocol 7.1, I should abort my involvement in the operation, but I thought it important that I continue to follow the situation in case of further developments.

I didn't have to wait long. After an interval, there was a stirring among the bodies; someone was moving, an arm flailing. It was deHoog. He'd been pinned by the bodyguards and was struggling to dig his way out from under them. I touched an index finger to the monitor, as if to help him.

And maybe this worked, because a moment later, one of the bodyguards stumbled to his feet, clutching a hand to his abdomen. There was a spreading stain on the back of his blazer, he appeared to be in a state of agitation. Seeing his downed companion, he knelt over him, as if in lamentation, he pulled at the man's shoulders, slapped his face as though to wake him. DeHoog, relieved of the weight, climbed out from under the body. He glanced around wildly, then staggered headlong into Suite 1801. I had no camera access to the suites, I couldn't see what happened in there, but sixty-odd seconds later, he rushed out again, lurched toward the elevators and, pounding a fist on the buttons, attempted to summon one. When none arrived, he ran out of frame toward, I suspect, the stairwell.

—*We have some familiarity with the events you've described, the what and the how, at least. But the why has eluded us. It appears that, given your position within the hotel, you have a unique perspective on your co-workers.*

—So I guess I'm of some small use, then. I feel often that people don't appreciate my contributions. It's people like Travis, my manager, it's people like him, they talk a good game, they know how to present themselves. It's people like that who get ahead. Travis is from the Humber College program, too, he graduated seven years behind me, but already he's a manager. He doesn't even care about the job, not the way he should, he has no passion for loss prevention, he just likes the title and the money. When the Company first approached me for recruitment, I thought about Travis, about how shocked he'd be if he knew that you'd approached me instead of him, the quiet girl, not the golden boy with the gleaming teeth. It would have eaten away at him. You saw something special in me, not Travis. And I don't know, maybe this was the reason, initially at least, I'd been interested in your project. The day before the operation, I'd overheard him talking on the phone. His tone was ingratiating, so I knew he was talking to a superior. A government official, or maybe just deHoog. He's an unctuous little know-nothing, if I'm being frank. "Let me reiterate," he said to the telephone, "I understand your concerns, but I assure you, the facility is airtight. We have an RFID locking system in place on all of the suites. It's fully integrated with the MM8000 danger-management application. The Siemens people were here just last week, updating the servers. Our staff is highly trained, sensitive to guest comfort, and responsive. I promise you that Mr. Linera's satisfaction is a priority for us, as is the comfort of all of our guests." When Travis ended the call, he closed his eyes, pinched the bridge of his nose. "I'm going down there," he said to Mohammed, "look after things here." He rushed out of the office. He always put Mohammed in charge, even though I had seniority, he didn't trust me, he didn't respect me. And now I felt a bright spark of joy, the avalanche of S-H-I-T that would inundate him. I'd be shocked if he wasn't fired for this, was he fired for this? Do you know? He'd had all his systems in place, his threat assessment was airtight, sure, but for one little oversight.

—*What was that?*

—Why, me, of course. Revenge of the nerd. It was approximately 3:45 by the time I'd verified the backups on the external drive, wiped the system clean of all activity from 2:30 p.m. to 3:30, sixty minutes in total, and then bundled the drive and my mobile in the Company-issued valise. I powered up the emergency alarms and rebooted the MM8000's security subsytem. Then I logged off and just walked out. The hotel was in a state of chaos. Toronto Police Service everywhere, security contractors shouting, VIPs from the breakfast banquet held on site, outraged, unable to leave. As I picked my way through the lobby, I saw an elderly couple, clearly in distress. The man had fallen to the floor, panting, hand clapped to his chest, the woman in her wheelchair leaning over him, "Clarence! Clarence!" Screaming into his face. I dashed to the front doors, exited the building. Two policemen were standing by the taxi rank, I smiled at them, but they didn't appear to register my presence. I strolled down the steps and onto the street and soon enough was on the express train to the airport, and Rendezvous Redtail. This was the end of my active participation in the operation.

—*Well, this has been a very thorough accounting, I appreciate you taking the — um, okay. Just a sec. You said active. Active participation. As opposed to …*

—Well, as I said before, I haven't exactly been working on my tan since I arrived here. I'm still convalescing from the effects of my neighbours' sonic attacks, even after all this time, so the work has been intermittent, but I've nevertheless managed to conduct a post-mortem of that disastrous day, and I think you'll be interested in my findings. I think they'll be helpful.

—*Uh-huh. And what have you found?*

—Well, to start, I know all about the Company. Believe me, this wasn't easy. The internet is throttled here, so it's slow going, but if you're determined, you can still get things done. There were layers and layers of obfuscation, you hid yourselves well. I started with a guess. The file names for your YouTube videos, DOWN7, and the branding on our monthly packages. I pulled on that thread, and eventually I discovered exactly one mention of the Seven Down Corporation on the r/JoeRogan subreddit. This was encouragement enough. I googled, I swept the image boards and forums. And what I found, over many months, was that the Seven Down Corporation was owned by SDC Holdings LLC, which was owned by Heptad Recovery Systems, which was owned by … you get the idea. Shell company upon shell company, it was mind-bending, puppets, filings with Panamanian regulators, I don't pretend to understand it all, dead links, deactivated phone numbers, soft 404 errors, but eventually I came upon it, who you really are, you're [Redacted], formerly [Redacted], a low-profile crisis management security consultancy known mostly for its involvement in a morally suspect and questionably motivated diplomatic incident in Tripoli, and currently in the midst of a hostile takeover by a hedge fund. But the good news is I have also uncovered information that can help you regain your equilibrium within your industry. I know who fouled up the operation.

—*Oh yes? Please don't keep me in suspense.*

—It was deHoog. Mr. deHoog, our manager of operations. He was the one I saw on Feed 18 coming out of the security suite with the two bodyguards.

—*Wow. And how did you come to that conclusion?*

—I did what I do. I put the pieces together. Think about it. What was Mr. deHoog doing on the very floor where Carlos Linera was staying? What possible business could he have had up there? Clearly he was part of the operation, there was no other reason. But why

would he sign on to be part of something like this? Motivation is the key piece here. He made good money at the King William, a six-figure salary. He lived in a large house in Oakville, not quite lakefront, but close. An attractive, credulous wife who didn't know or didn't care about all of the sex he was having with other men's attractive wives. He had two handsome children destined for achievement. He coached soccer. Why would he give all of that up? It doesn't make sense. Unless you factor in his so-called spiritual life. According to all of the accounts that I've come across — his "obituary," for instance, not that he's really dead — deHoog was, or is, a devout fellow, active in the Catholic community, he was a genuine church-head. What does that have to do with the price of milk? Well, nothing, unless you consider the various conferences he attended from at least the fall of 2012 to at least the summer of 2014, all of them documented online. They were billed as faith-building conferences, designed to promote God-centred learning experiences, organized by the Western Interfaith Alliance. They took place in a series of hotels across North America. He spoke at these conferences on a variety of panels, on a number of different topics of concern, along with clergy and other business and community leaders. How is this significant? Because of the considerable overlap he had on these panels with another speaker, one Arthur Schultz. Who is Arthur Schultz? Well, he is no one if not the executive director of the North American Council of Churches. Do you see now?
—*Uh-huh. No. I'm afraid I'm not getting it.*
—The NACC, I thought everyone knew this, the NACC was and is a front organization for the CIA.
—*That's ... quite incredible.*
—Yes, so, but you see, my point is, this is what I can bring to the Company — indefatigable research and an eye for the telling detail. I assume you know about my father.
—*Uh, should I?*

SEVEN DOWN

—It must be in my file.

—*I've only just had a chance to skim your file.*

—My father died mysteriously when I was a child. This really should be in my file. It's an event that was both a foundational trauma in my life, and a critical moment in my development. A father and a daughter have a special kind of bond, and ours was no different. He doted on me, I adored him. I remember the picnics we went on, the pony rides, the gifts, no reason, no birthday. One day he brought me a Wonder Woman doll, this was the seventies, he knew I idolized Lynda Carter. But it was all fated to end, this idyllic childhood, one terrible day when my mother, Judith, called me in, I was outside playing in the backyard, to tell me that Daddy had died. "What do you mean?" I said. I knew "died" of course, I understood the concept, I'd flushed my guppy Chico not six months before. I meant how, and why. "He fell," my mother said, "from a height. Because he was sad," she said. "Why was he sad?" I said. He'd never struck me as being especially sad, he liked to smoke his pipe, and sing along to Johnny Paycheck, and watch *The Rockford Files*. The only static in his life was the shouting matches he had with my mother, the bellowed accusations, the content of which I don't remember or have blocked out. Anyway, a few weeks after he died, Mother's friend Burt started coming round the house, always with a bottle of Mateus and a Wunderbar for me. Their visits grew more frequent. Eventually Burt stopped swinging by, because he was never not there. I don't know how much time passed. And then one morning Mother and her friend and I had a conversation about how I should stop calling him Mr. Cannon and start calling him Father. I was an observant child; the confluence of these two incidents was not lost on me. Daddy might indeed have fallen from a height, but Judith and Burt, it was obvious to me, had given him a nudge. All of which is to say that I learned from a very young age not to trust events on their face. Always dig deeper. And it's these kinds of intangibles, soft skills, if you will, that make me so effective in my work.

—*You can be sure I'll pass this along to my supervisor.*

—Thank you. I can't stand to be idle. This place is a gilded cage. It's picturesque, I concede, and temperate, the winters are particularly pleasant, but it's so quiet. There was a time in Toronto I would have longed for this peace, but now that I have it, it's … lonely. I don't have any friends here. Even Travis, god help me, would be a welcome companion. I try to make conversation with the lady who runs the bakery, but she hardly seems to notice me. At night, there's something I do now, to fall asleep, I shouldn't be telling you this, I record myself on this old, I guess you'd call it a vintage cassette player I bought at one of the markets here. I speak into it, I talk about my day, or whatever's on my mind at the time. And then I play it back. I lie in bed, listening to the warbled recording of my own voice, until I drift off. And if I imagine hard, I can pretend it's someone else, a friend, a lover, cooing to me while I doze, and it makes me, I don't know, less alone somehow.

I'm still convalescing, certain central nervous system effects, vestibular issues, I'm at loose ends, I don't know what to do with myself. I'm out of sorts.

Out here in this unfamiliar place, this sweet little island. Nothing's the same out here. The language, the food. The salty weather, the squalls that blow in off the sea. Even the wall sockets are funny. Nothing works here. Nothing works the way you think it ought to work.

END OF TRANSCRIPTION
PREPARED AND SUBMITTED BY: AL-AZMAH, A.

C O N F I D E N T I A L [UNDISCLOSED LOCATION] 008393
DEPARTMENT FOR NEA/I
SUBJECT: CORRECTED COPY: ASSET INTERVIEW

REF: A. [UNDISCLOSED LOCATION] 5489
Classified By: CDA Officer Y.L. Zhèng for reasons: 4.0 (a)–(d).

ASSET ID: "MANAGEMENT" [Legal name Rodney deHoog]
March 7, 2022 — 15:11 EST

Day of Operation Fear and Trembling

—You are Support, aren't you? Who are you, exactly? Are you Support? I need to talk to Winnifred. I need to talk to my wife. Are you Support? What do you think you're doing? Why am I wearing a seat belt? Where are we going? I need to talk to my, I think I'm, I think I've been, who are you people? I've been in a terrible —
— *[Inaudible.]*
—What?
—*[Inaudible.]*
—I did everything you told me to do, but the chutney was a loss. I can't breathe. I have, I have shortness of breath. I did everything you said, down to the ladder. The letter. I need to talk to my wife. Good lord, where are we? That park. Wait, wait, wait, wait, I know that park, it's where Winnifred and I first stop, the car, I need to get, do you hear me? Does he hear me? You tell him to stop, the car, I'll get out this, next set of lights. It's okay, I, can walk back to —
—*[Inaudible.]*

—I don't know. Everything was, was, was fine we, were just pushing buttons, Enter, Escape, but then the rain started, an inundation, a deluge. I did what you said.

—*[Inaudible.]*

—Both of them, yes. Both, both were there. We had gathered in the suite, and I have to get out now. Can you hear me? I have terrible injuries and I think I might, I think I'm going to die. Do you hear me? I have to get to a hospital before I —

—*[Inaudible.]*

—You can't be serious. I have to get to a, you're not listening. No, I won't calm down. I have to get to a, what's that thing you're? What's in there? What are you going to do? It's in my file, I don't like needles. You must know I don't like —

—*Please, Mr. deHoog, try to [inaudible].*

—Calm down, he says. No, no, no, I won't calm down. This is not a time for effing calm. I'm about to, do you hear me? I'm worried that I might succumb to my, this is a, how do you say it? This is a dying man's statement. I want to speak with my wife. I want to speak with Winnifred.

—*[Inaudible.]*

—Are you sure you're Support? What is it with you? You're all the-the-the same. I did everything I was told to do. I was in the security suite with Thing One and Thing Two. I did everything you, and we were. But the rain, not the rain, no, the, he had a gun. The bellman with the blurry face, his eyes were wild, a cornered dog, he had a gun, he shot at me. Do you understand this, have you, yourself been shot at? He pulled out his gun and everyone was shouting through the rain and the thunder cracks were deafening and I thought I'd go deaf and I thought I would die right there on the broadloom and I want to speak to my wife now. No, I won't. No, no, no, I won't. Get — stop it. Don't touch me with, that thing, I — Jesus, Jesus, Jesus.

[*Unintelligible comments redacted.*]

SEVEN DOWN

◆ ◆ ◆

March 7, 2022 — 15:21 EST

—*Mr. deHoog? How are you feeling?*
—Much better, thank you. I'm, thank you. I'm sorry.
—*[Redacted], have you fixed the audio? Okay, good. All right, I'm sorry, Mr. deHoog, but I'm hoping you can tell me what happened. I'm afraid it's quite urgent.*
—Oh, sure. Oh yes, I can do that. Can you hear me? I can't tell if you can hear me, my ears are plugged, it feels as if I'm speaking through a pane of glass. Walk you through it, yessir, I can do that. Just let me gather my, mm-hmm. I was sitting in my office. This was before the owl. Just give me a, this morning. I'll think back. My office at home, yes, not at work. It was early, before dawn. Everyone else was asleep. Winnifred sleeps late, and the kids don't get up till just before school. Caden and Olivia, nine and eleven. Funny at that age. I got your message on Twitter, then the YouTube clip, the swaying palms, they reminded me of Aruba. So that's how I found out today was the day. I wasn't nervous or sad, if you can believe it. Or maybe a little bit, but mostly I was in reasonable spirits. I'd been looking forward to this day, in a way I can't quite articulate, looking forward to what was waiting for me. Something new. I do love novelty. Curious about what would be required of me, how it would all play out. An adventure in an otherwise unremarkable life. I put on my nicest tie to mark the occasion, a light-blue Brooks Brothers, seven-fold silk. Do you like it? It cost me a pretty — oh shit. Look at that, is that a, that's a bullethole, isn't it?
—*I'm afraid we don't have a great deal of time. So maybe if we could try to stay on topic.*
—Of course. Of course. Apologies. It's just that it cost me an arm and a, never mind. I'm sorry, friend, don't mind me. So where was

I. Your message. Start there? *Greetings from Copenhagen.* Yes. What the heck, I thought when I saw it. Why are they sending me a post-card? But I didn't have time to consider the question. I got up and got dressed and put on this dumb tie that is now beyond dry cleaning and put out the Honey Smacks for the kids. I tried not to think about the kids. And when that was all done, I spent a few minutes saying goodbye to the house. Goodbye, golf clubs. Goodbye, TV remote. I know it sounds goofy, but I get attached to objects; it's like they're sentient, like they're going to miss me. When you're alive, all the objects you accumulate, all the wristwatches and floor lamps, all your good china, photos and books and favourite sweaters, they float around you like the moons around Saturn. And then when you die, and your gravity is gone, all that stuff is flung out into the charity shops and estate sales, other people's drawers, and they turn inanimate once more. All their meaning, their meaning is gone. Goodbye, sectional sofa, where I watched all those grand slam tennis finals, where I curled up with my kids in the winter, where I spread out when I was sick — you sure were good to me. I didn't say goodbye to my family, lest I arouse suspicion. I prowled around the house, in the dark, that one final time. And then I was gone. My last trip down the QEW. SportsTalk 1010 on the car radio. As I passed Cawthra Road, I looked out the window and caught a glimpse of our church, the steeple flashing by. St. Mary's Catholic. And for the first time then I felt a little throb of what was it. Not sadness. Not sadness, exactly. Wistfulness. Our first kiss had been in that church. In the utility room off of the Sunday school, where they keep all the soccer balls. There'd been an event that day for the kids. Corn dogs and three-legged races and the sky, I'll never forget the sky. This depthless blue. Like a, the words es-cape me. Cerulean. Like the Sistine Chapel. The colour of heaven. The air smelled of grass clippings. I'd gone into the utility room to get some stacking chairs for the potluck, and someone coughed, and when I turned around, there she was, in the doorway, suffused in a golden glow, the slanting sunlight through the window, those almondine eyes. She'd followed me in there.

"I thought you could use another set of hands," she said.

She'd intended this as innuendo, but I pretended not to get it.

"Oh sure," I said. I didn't know what to say. "Sure, great," I said.

"I saw you stealing glances at me," she said, "when you were over by the condiment station."

"Was I?" I said — so stupid, so inadequate. "I'm sorry," I said, "I didn't realize."

She shut the door behind her. "The reason I noticed was because I was looking right back at you," she said. "I've been looking back at you for weeks."

Her hair was a wild blond mane. I mean, you have to understand. The women of St. Mary's don't have hair like that. Overflowing. Brighter than is natural. She was lanky, too, like a volleyball centre. Everything about her was a testament to abundance. I desired her, oh yes, I thirsted for that woman, but you know what I did? I shook my head no.

I told her that Winnifred was just outside. I stammered as I said it. I asked her what about her husband, and her kids, they were just outside. She shut her eyes like she had shut the door and said that this was about us, not them.

—*Please, Mr. deHoog, if we could just please stay on topic.*

—You're right, of course you're right. I'm just remembering. You don't need to know all my secrets. It's just a happy thing for — me at this time. Never mind. This morning was uneventful. A couple on the fifteenth floor was aggrieved by all the extra security. They felt uncomfortable, they couldn't move freely. I assured them the inconvenience was temporary, that there were some famous guests staying at the hotel, they'd soon be gone, and that I'd speak to all the relevant parties. They were primly dressed, this couple, a touch snappish, they were used to having their way. Our guests expect service, they're willing to pay for it. You can't let yourself get rattled. At 12:30, I went to lunch. I treated myself to a roast beef and Yorkshire pudding and a half glass of Guinness at the pub down the block. I sat alone at the table and tucked in, and thought to myself, Rod, this is your last Canadian meal.

Two hours earlier, 10:30 a.m., my burner had rung. I'd been sitting in my office, door shut, waiting. "Greetings from Copenhagen," the woman on the phone had said. "The gardens are abundant," I told her. In a wintery monotone, she directed me to, quote, proceed to the Royal Suites, room 1801, at precisely 2:35. She emphasized precision. Precision was key, that I should consult only my Company-issued smart watch. She explained what it was that I was to do, and I was a tad surprised, I will confess. How simple my assignment was. No laptops to hack. No locks to pick. Nothing to activate or deactivate. Nothing that would draw upon anything other than the skill set of a highly trained hospitality administrator. I snickered, I did, like the village fool, alone at my desk. "Proceed to the Royal Suites," she said, "eighteenth floor." Of course I knew who was staying in that suite. It was my business to know, and now it was my business not to have an opinion. Just do what I was told and keep my yap shut. And whosoever shall exalt himself shall be abased, and he that shall humble himself shall be exalted. And it's not even that I hate her, you understand? Winnifred. I feel … not pity, not pity. Sympathy. We were so young when we were married, just out of college. You barely know yourself when you're that young, much less who you'll turn into. I'd met her at George Brown. She was in Design, I was in Hospitality. Her parents were these almost comically uptight WASPs, they lived in Leaside, naturally. Her father was an engineer, he designed underpasses. They thought she was slumming it with me, the ginger-haired dork in the U2 T-shirt. We'd sit in their tasteful living room armchairs and drink Constant Comment and talk about the room that surrounded us. "That piece," she'd say, Winnifred's mother, "that piece," she'd call it. "We picked up that piece at this pretty little shop in Yorkville" and "I am not happy with these throw pillows" and "I am thinking of repainting this spring." I'd joke about it later, when Winnifred and I were alone. And she'd slap at my arm and stifle a giggle and say, "I know, I know, be kind, their house is all they have in common anymore." And I'd growl like a bear and wrap my arms around her and we'd drive back to our little flat and have sex and I'd stare up at the ceiling feeling something I thought was contentment. Little did I know. Fifteen years later, our friends are over, one occasion or another, we're sitting on our tasteful living room furniture talking about our tasteful living room furniture. You can't outrun your destiny.

—*Here, have some water.*

—Do I need water?

—*Please, drink it. You'll feel better.*

[*Subject drinks from water bottle.*]

—Oh yes, oh yes, you are so right. This is ... my gosh, some of the finest water I've ever ... Like an alpine stream. Like the streams that feed Lake Superior.

—*So, to continue. You were telling us about what happened at the hotel.*

—The hotel, of course, yes. What happened at the hotel. Of course. I was on my way to the Royal Suites and it's not that I ever intended to cheat on her, Winnifred, my wife, I wasn't happy, no, but I could cope, I could cope. It was a velvet discontent. I had my TV. I had my whatnot, my outdoor grill. The affair lasted three years. It wasn't an affair. I loved her. I would've slit a goat's throat to be with her. An odour of a sweet smell, a sacrifice acceptable, well pleasing to God. Philippians. I know how it sounds, I don't really mean it, except that I do. Every Wednesday and Saturday we'd meet in a parking lot, we'd meet at a hotel. We'd eat dinner in a different part of town. Pho in Etobicoke, fasolatha on the Danforth. My shield-maiden, I called her. From old Norse mythology. On Sundays, we'd see each other at church and pray not for guidance, nor for redemption, but for some way to redraw reality, erase our families and obligations. Three years living like this. And then she ended it, on a cold afternoon in November. Lowering sky, like a painting, metallic grey, unquiet clouds, dead leaves rotting at the curbsides. We were sitting in my car in Sunnyside Park. "We can't continue," she told me, "there are children involved. I've been thinking about this, I won't change my mind. We have to be strong. Maybe in the next life," she said. "In the next life we'll be together." She was sobbing. It felt like she'd punched a hole in my chest and sucked out my soul. "I don't care about the next life," I said, "I only care about you." "You don't mean that," she said. But I did, I did. And I still do. Whatever that stuff was you gave me, the pain is now completely gone, thank you. I feel much restored.

At 2:35 precisely, I stepped out of the elevators onto the eighteenth floor. These were the Royal Suites. Four in total, all of them booked for the convention by Mr. Linera and his entourage, they took up the entire floor. "There will be two bodyguards," my contact had said, "stationed at Mr. Linera's door." What she hadn't told me was how terrifying they'd be. Two goliaths, six cubits and a span, stuffed into off-the-rack Hugo Boss suits. One had his head shaved, these thick rolls of neck fat tucked into the back of his collar; the other slicked back his hair like a stockbroker from the nineties, a serpentine deadness to his eyes, a painful-looking razor burn on his throat. Both had Bluetooth receivers plugged into their ears like implants, like the bolts in the neck of Frankenstein's monster. "Apologize for the inconvenience," my contact had said.

"The security feeds will be down; inform them of this unfortunate situation."

"Gentlemen," I said, "I'm afraid we're having an issue with our security feeds and —" no, no, no, no, no. Why are you? Where are we going? The hospitals are the other way. There's nothing. You're heading east. There's nothing east. Why is he? Oh good God, you're going to let me just bleed out, right here in the back of a Subaru, aren't you? Oh, come on, you can't kid a kidder. I know what you, I know a lie when I hear it. No, no, no, stop it. I'm fine. Not another, please, not anoth—

[*Unintelligible comments redacted.*]

◆ ◆ ◆

March 7, 2022 — 15:45 EST

—*Mr. deHoog. Can you hear me?*

—Sorry, I think I nodded off. I was having the loveliest dream. She was wearing a leather catsuit, like a blond Diana Rigg. She told me she couldn't keep —

—*Could you, if I could get you to focus for a second. Can you follow my finger? Do you know where you are?*

—Mm-hmm, yes. I'm inside a Subaru. It's getting dark.

—*Do you remember what happened today?*

—Oh yes. I went to work, I took the kids to hockey. I walked the dog at 5:30 in the morning when the sky was pitch-black and drizzling. I filled out tax forms, I took the car in for twice-yearly maintenance. I attended the weddings of in-laws I disliked. I sat through assemblies of public school children flailing on their wind instruments. I spent endless hours supervising birthday parties at Chuck E. Cheese. I mowed thousands of miles of lawn, hauled hundreds of tons of household waste. I paid bills, I paid bills, I paid bills. Gas and hydro and water and phone and cable. I bought a home, I got a mortgage. I sat down once a year with a guy who pitched me his insurance plans. In the event of my death, in case of dismemberment. I bought RRSPs and RESPs and GICs and TFSAs. I was a conscientious husband, a kind and thoughtful father. I provided. I scoured the sinks and scrubbed the tub and folded the laundry. I did what was asked of me.

—*Sir, I need you to focus. Do you hear me? I need you to tell me what happened today at the hotel. It's extremely important.*

—Yes, yes. This morning, some guests, a couple on the fifteenth floor. They were not happy. They complained about the precautions, the inconvenience. I told you this? I had to reassure them. That the disruptions were transient. I already told you this. Later, on the way back from my pub lunch, I spotted them. They were stopped at a crosswalk; I caught up to them and eavesdropped. "I could not get into the pool," the man said. "I could not do my laps." The old woman hugged her satchel to her side. "What is the purpose of a platinum membership when they treat us like that?" she said. "That awful bellboy, he looked at me like he had something better to do with his day. We might as well have booked into a Travelodge."

Well, when I heard this nonsense, I couldn't help myself. You know me, you know my file. I have no politics, no strong opinions. But I snorted and I scoffed and I didn't worry if they heard it. We work tirelessly to provide world-class accommodations for our guests, our mission is not only to meet but to exceed desecrations. The man, he turned and, what did I say? Expectations. Exceed expectations. You cannot malign my team members without getting a reaction from me, on that you can depend. The gentleman turned his attention briefly toward me, but seemed not to remember he'd just wasted half an hour of my life with his bitching and bellyaching. The lights changed and we parted ways. Forever, as it turns out. I won't be seeing them again, lucky for me. There is a last time for everything. Thank God you don't know it. Every moment of the day, the end of something, the beginning of something else. My second affair was with a woman named — no, I won't tell you her name. We met at the HAC conference. The hotel association. In the afternoon plenary session, day two. Oh screw it, her name was Sherry, what do I care. She was sitting with a mutual acquaintance. They invited me for cocktails after that evening's panel, and I don't know what happened, I had one too many martinis, one minute we're chatting at the bar, the next I'm in her suite on my knees tearing off her panties with my teeth. "I could get used to this," she told me later, when we were done. She said, "My husband only cares about his Callaways." Her husband works in marketing, he prefers golf to sex.

A descendance into the, the, the fleshly, the fleshly otherance. She wasn't even my type. I don't know why I did what I did. Yes, I do. I was a steadfast man. I did everything I was supposed to do. I was owed something, it had seemed to me, so I took my prize while still upon the earth, I didn't feel like waiting. The flesh, the flesh, the thighs, the soft underside of the arm, the neck where you nuzzle it. The great cosmos owed me this. She treated me well, she was enthusiastic in bed, so I managed to, I don't know how to say it. Fetishize. Her little imperfections. She had a raised pink scar where a surgeon had excised her appendix. I thought about that scar, too much, at work, I sent her lecherous texts. It ended badly, in the rain, three months later. She'd developed what I felt to be an abnormal attachment. She got it into her head that somehow we were meant for each other, that we should acknowledge this fact and should tell our others. I'd get these reply texts, these emails. She couldn't let go of the idea. We were sitting in my Audi, in a parking garage across from Harbourfront Centre. The rain was raining down. "I'm sorry," I said.

"I can't believe you'd do this to us," she said, after a protracted silence. "After everything we've went through." Gone through.

And I'm thinking, gone through? It's been three months, I've been with Winnifred for eighteen years. Now that — that is quote, unquote gone through. But I kept shtum, lest the situation spiral. I hugged her and pretended to choke down tears and said I couldn't do this to my kids, and she had no choice but to say she understood because, after all, she'd seem like just the worst person if she didn't. I forced her into that, this was my gambit, if she were that selfish there'd be no chance that I'd regret or reconsider, she was playing the long game, and there it was, how little she knew me. Of course I could do that to my kids, why not? If the woman was right.

There was one time, my wife. She was sitting at the kitchen table, muesli and a pamphlet, before work, she's a customer success manager at a large retail clothing chain. And she turns to me, this deep crease running down the middle of her forehead, and says, "I am buying you an urn." I ask her to repeat herself. "An urn," she says, "a burial urn." And I say, "Well, that's a little premature, don't you think?" Trying to make a joke. And she just sighs and stares out the window, she's exasperated, and says, "I never could stand those drapes." And I don't know what I say then and I don't know how I got there, but that night I find myself drinking more than one Coors Light at Browne's Tap and Grill, a sports bar down on the Queensway. Monday Night Football, Lions versus Vikings. I couldn't shake the thought of it, that burial urn. Winnifred in the kitchen, contemplating my ashy remains. The way the soul flattens, goes limp. It starts out as this bouncing balloon, but over time succumbs to all the pinpricks, all the little insults that allow the gas to escape. I won't need that urn, though, will I? That's the funny part. You'll be dumping me into the ocean, won't you, boys, or tossing me into a ditch full of quicklime like they did with the Romanovs. That's not, I don't mind. That's not a dig. I don't care what you do with this shell once I've sloughed it off. It's what happens next, when the rest of me roams free, that's what matters. I'll be waiting up in the great golden hall for my shield-maiden to join me. Oh, Winnifred. I've been so weak. So self-indulgent.

—*Mr. deHoog. It is imperative that you hear me. We do not have much time. I need you to resume your narrative of the day. Can you do that?*

—Well, sure. Where did we leave things?

—*You were on the eighteenth floor.*

—Of course. At 2:35 precisely, I stepped out of the elevators on the eighteenth floor, where I came across two gargantuan bodyguards.

"Gentlemen," I said, "I'm afraid we're having an issue with our security feeds." Mr. Linera's bodyguards just stared, I was afraid they spoke only Spanish. I pressed on. "There appears," I said, "to be a widespread outage affecting certain of our older cameras. I'm told it has something to do with the March security patch. Our team is looking into it, and we expect to have it resolved momentarily. We don't believe it's affecting the cameras on this floor, but I'd like, out of an abundance of caution, to check the monitors in the security suite."

The security suite, so-called, was a makeshift setup in the room adjacent to Carlos Linera's rooms, a bank of monitors tied into our main Loss Prevention network, our entire CCTV, and a receiver that pulled audio from Mr. Linera's security staff.

They murmured words to each other, Spanish and English, I made out half: *mierda*, they said, *lastimoso*. I don't know what they said. In time, though, my guileless demeanour trumped their professional skepticism, and they led me into the security suite.

—*Mierda? That's it? Are you sure you didn't hear anything else?*

—Well, what is certainty? I was anxious. My blood was pulsing in my ears. You're lucky I noticed anything at all. Can you even guess the stress I was under?

—Not having been in your position, I can only guess. A significant amount of stress?

—Well, yes, because one of them seemed to be smiling. The one, I don't know how to describe him. With the fat shaved head. A lunacy in his eyes, he was born to be a bodyguard. I guess that's how I would — wait, where are we going? This is the, we're on the Don Valley? Where could we be —

—Mr. deHoog, if you could try to focus.

—No, you focus. I'm perfectly, I'm as focused as I'll ever be. You can't just, I need to speak to Winnifred. My phone. I need to tell her. To ignore that goddamn letter. It's all been a lie. All this time I've been looking for escape routes. Losing myself in one thing or another.

Lions versus Vikings. Sitting at the sports bar on the Queensway, four Coors Lights in, plate of wings, suicide on the side. This rumpled guy sitting beside me. "Slay's been a monster this season," he says. This was back when Darius Slay was on the team. I smile and nod. Rumpled guy's wearing a Bills jersey, big gut, lined face, needs a shave. "You a Lions fan?" he says. "Grew up in Windsor," I say. He nods, he gets it. Male shorthand. Tribal allegiances, secret handshakes. Outside, the street is frigid, the wind off the lake, skeletons of leaves skittering down the sidewalk. Three men by the door having a smoke. "The wife let you out for the night?" the rumpled guy says. He's nodding at my ring finger. I give him a polite smile, he's wearing thin already. "If you marry, you will regret it," he says. "If you don't marry, you will also regret it." I pretend not to hear him. "Men, they need to roam," he says, "women often don't understand this. We need a long leash. That's what keeps us around." Please, just shut up, I think, but I don't say anything. The Lions D get a takeaway, offence takes over, two minutes later they score seven points, this game is as good as done. I down the rest of my pint, pull out my wallet. My neighbour says, "How long have you been cheating on your wife, Rodney?" I freeze. A disruption overtakes me, a deep nausea that seeps into every fibre and sinew. He knows my name. I don't dare look at him, I just fix my gaze upon the rows of glowing bottles, rums and ryes, behind the bar. Neon beer signs, framed baseball jerseys. And wait for whatever it is that's coming.

"There are bad fellas out there," he says after a while. "Lots of them. Who want to do real harm on a large scale. When you fuck around on your wife, who are you hurting? Maybe your honey, but beyond that? It's your business as far as I go, doesn't make you a bad guy. Good men sleep around when they're unhappy, when they feel neglected, or when they need a way out of a shit situation. They're not out to hurt anyone, are they? They're up-standing citizens, leaders in faith and community. But maybe they have families. Maybe they have reasons why they don't want their personal business to become public knowledge. Maybe they go to some lengths to keep that from happening. Or maybe, maybe it's not about them at all, maybe they feel they need to protect the folks they care about. I don't know. What do you say?"

I don't respond. The flat screen in front of me has morphed into a piece of abstract art, smears and blurs and blocks of florid colour. I force myself to look at him. His eyes are full of what? Malice? Concern? Sorrow? Sincerity? I can't read it. He smiles, the lines around his eyes deepen into ruts. "Tell you what," he says, "have a seat, I'm going to buy you a beer."

And that's the way it happened. Four years ago now, hard to believe. That's how I came to work for you guys. At first I — how is Mona, by the way? God, she makes me chuckle. Those owl eyes, the lenses in her glasses. Does she know about this?

—*I can't say for certain. Events are unfolding.*

—Someone should tell her, I think she likes me. At first I was cross, I don't mind telling you. The way you guys operate? I felt pretty messed with. The choice you gave me was not a choice at all, it was blackmail. But with time, I started to see the positives. The dirty trick you played, it mutated and shifted in my mind until I saw it for what it really was. A gift. God chooses His instruments slyly, and in this instance He chose as His cudgel a doofus in a Buffalo Bills jersey. With all my options gone, all the angst, all the wrestling with the wrong or the right, it was gone, too. And at the perfect time, because I'd just begun my third extramarital, and the way things were going, the rapids I was racing down, it wasn't going to end well. I was getting reckless, mixing the personal and the professional. It was like I wanted to be found out, who I really was exposed for all to see. She was a guest at the hotel. Her name was, screw it, I'll tell you, you probably already know, her name was Chelsea. A pharmaceutical rep from Syracuse, New York. Every couple of months, she'd stay at the hotel for five nights, Sunday to Thursday. I'd go up to her room after work and we'd, you know. There was nothing to it at all, nothing but carnal needs. I told her nothing about myself. She didn't ask. Our conversation consisted of preferred positions, and what we'd like for room service, and the weather outside. I lie. One time we talked about Syria, or Chechnya, or the USA, something in the news, I really can't remember. She said it was a terrible situation, whatever it was. We were having a glass of something red, Zinfandel, lounging on the bed in hotel robes and — where are we, anyway? Is that? That's mutton full air whore. What did I say? Buttonville. Buttonville Airport. Are we boarding a plane? More than once I'd — are we going somewhere? More than once I'd wondered if this woman, this Chelsea in quotation marks, was a contractor for the Company. It all seemed too convenient. This attractive woman, offering perfunctory, workmanlike sex, around just often enough to serve as a pressure valve, and to keep me from seeking out other releases. And also the perfect blackmail material for the Company's initial approach. I could see where all this was heading, and it was disconcerting. My increasingly bold behaviour. The next logical step would be a co-worker. I'd catch myself considering it, the savage part of my mind working behind the scenes while the civilized part was somewhere else. I'd be out in the lobby, talking to my assistant GM or someone else, and out the side of my eye I'd spy a woman-shaped blur, and I'd glance over reflexively, and I'd start to stammer, I'd lose the capacity to speak, such was my desire. There was one in particular. The brunette on front desk. Gosh, what I wouldn't have given for just one night. She was — what's the word? No word quite works. I'd met her once at a staff function, I forget which. She told me she was from up north, near Lake Superior. I loved the way those words made me feel. I pictured dark water, black rocks, Precambrian magma. They smelled of pine, those words. There was something about her, we were connected somehow, I don't know how. But of course I wasn't stupid, I knew also that after it was over with her there would have been others, an endless string of them, that's where this river would have stranded me, and the thought of it left me empty and cold, and that's why when I sat down in my office at home this morning and scrolled through Twitter and saw @unfavorablesemicircle's tweet, I laughed. I'm serious, I laughed, that was my reaction. I saw my reflection in the toaster, the distorted funhouse smile. I'd been saved from myself. My son, do not regard lightly the discipline of the Lord, nor be weary when we're reproved by Him. For the Lord disciplines the one He loves, and chastises every son whom He receives. We've stopped. Are we? This isn't the right airport. Where are you taking me?

—*Road closures. Construction on the 401. We were forced to divert.*

—I need to call my wife.

—*Of course. But first we need your statement.*

—Please let me call my wife.

—Absolutely, but first we need you to give us all the information you can.

—Yes, yes, yes. Fine, fine, fine. Then you'll let me call my wife. You will. You will. Where was I. Yes, yes, the eighteenth floor. The two bodyguards, yes. Thing One and Thing Two.

Eventually my guileless manner trumped their professional skepticism, and they followed me into the security suite. The suite was just a normal room into which an improvised arrangement of computers had been stuffed side by side on catering tables, a tangle of wires spilling out beneath. The first bodyguard — Thing One, with the shaved head — seeing static on the monitors, the camera feeds down, stepped forward and began pressing keys on the keyboards, F5, Enter, Escape, I don't even know. Distract them for five minutes, my contact had said. So I told the bodyguards my best people were busy installing the patch, not to worry, I asked them if there was anything I could get for them, some coffee, a sandwich, I complimented them on their professionalism, I rattled on nonsensically, managed to distract them for a couple of minutes, when a fire alarm sounded, and the overhead sprinklers activated. "What the fuck?" Thing Two said. Excuse my language, but that's what he said. He squinted up at the sprinkler, then over at Thing One, and then they both looked at me, as if I were the cause of all of this. "Is this a system-wide intervention, or is it isolated to this floor?" Thing One said. I shrugged. I had no clue what was happening. No one told me about a fire alarm, I had no script for this.

In tandem, the two behemoths bolted from the security suite and thundered down the hallway. After a moment's, I will admit, a moment's hesitation, I followed, I had no idea what else to do. In the hallway, I saw the two bodyguards, sidearms drawn, shouting into the entrance of Suite 1801, Carlos Linera's room. I came up beside them, it was all so chaotic, but I caught a glimpse, for just one fraction of a second, inside the suite, of a bellman, I didn't know him, you can't know who everyone is, a hotel this size. His eyes were wild, I remember his frightened black eyes, he had an arm around Carlos Linera's throat, both were soaked under the sprinklers, he was using him as a shield. He said, "Back away, back away!" as he pointed his sidearm toward us.

"Put the gun down! Put the gun down!" the bodyguards bellowed.

And then the air began to shred, the very air, sliced apart like a sharp knife through silk, reality itself torn into ribbons, drifting to our feet. And then a one-two punch, first Thing One and then Thing Two, one then the other doubled over, grunting. Then I got it, too, a wet smack in the belly, and we all three toppled over onto our backs in a wild tumble.

A moment of. Peace. Just then. I was.

I was lying on a bed of moss, on a forest floor. Where was I? I knew this place, although I didn't know how. The green leafy gloom, the birdsong. Soft pellets of rain breaking through the canopy, splattering my face. Deep in the distance an owl was calling my name: "deHoog!" it said, "deHoog!" I was pinned by something heavy, immovable, the trunk of a fallen oak, I suspected, but little did I care, really, I was perfectly happy just to lie there listening to the forest creatures frolic, no past or future, no worries, no pain.

And then I snapped out of it. I wasn't in a forest glade, I was on my back on the hallway floor, staring up at the overhead sprinkler. I was indeed, as it turned out, pinned by a great weight, but it was the gasping and gurgling bulk of Thing One. Thing Two, lifting him by the shoulders, rolled him off of me, onto his back. Thing Two himself was clutching a hand to his abdomen; a dark geyser of blood pulsed through his fingers.

"After seven minutes precisely," my phone friend had said, "the feeds will resolve. Apologize once again, then walk calmly to the elevator and ride it back to street level. Exit the building through the service doors. Go to Union Station. Proceed via public transit to Rendezvous Kestrel." It was all very simple. Hard to believe I'd be compensated so generously for such a simple job. I leaned over Thing One. His chest was heaving. His eyes flicked back and forth, up at Thing Two, over at me, up to the ceiling, hopeless. He was trapped now, lost inside the prison of his flesh. Thing Two shouted words into his face. "Dear God," I said, "dear God." In a moment, I realized Thing Two was barking words at me, too. Something about something, something about something. Then suddenly the words broke through. "Medical!" he said. "You have medical! Call medical!"

"Yes, yes, I'll call them!" I said.

I stumbled upward and lurched into the suite. Blood splatter on the back wall, a service cart upended. The bellman was splayed out on the broadloom, his arms and legs akimbo, he had one bullet wound to his chest, another bullet had chewed off his neck. A container of chutney lay between his legs, lidless, a shattered vial inside, the contents dribbling out, but it didn't look like chutney to me, not at all, it was colourless and viscous, it smelled like rotten fruit.

—*All right, [Redacted], send a message to Regional. Tell them the guest was not, repeat, not served the chutney. Those exact words. Mr. deHoog, this is very important. Did you come into contact with the contents of the chutney container?*

—No, no. Hell no. I didn't have a chance, it was all too chaotic.

—*You're absolutely certain?*

—Well, now you're making me doubt myself. Why, what was in the chutney jar?

—*Never mind, nothing of any consequence. Please. You were saying.*

—I was saying, yes. I was saying. It was all so chaotic. Someone was shouting in my direction. I looked up to see Carlos Linera wielding a floor lamp as if it were a machete. An animal look in his eyes, he was certain I was there to harm him. There was something I was supposed to do, but I was forgetting. A protocol for this.

When an operation goes pear-shaped. I couldn't remember, and then I did: abort. I said something to Mr. Linera, I forget what, something to soothe him. Then backed out of the room, stepped over the bleeding heap of bodyguards, staggered to the stairwell, and spiralled down seventeen flights. When I reached the lobby everything was spinning. The guests, the staff. They spun around me, horses on a carousel. I made my way toward Receiving. People were staring, I was slathered in another man's blood. I tried to open the service door but it was locked. I screamed at a Receiving clerk to open it. He just stared at me and stuttered: his leader, his GM, sweat-soaked, bloody, ranting at him deliriously. I threw myself out the door and stumbled down the sidewalk, everything still spinning. I tripped over a homeless guy, I knocked into a busker. I pushed through some late-lunching business types as I ran without thinking toward Union Station. When I reached Front Street, I pushed between two parked taxis and stepped into the road and felt the earth scooped out from under me. I was flying, Henry. Floating through the air. Until two seconds later? Five months? Seven years? I dropped back down and landed in a bed made of crushed ice. I gazed up at the sky, it was full of glinting swords, hilts and tangs and pommels. I had just a moment to understand that I was lying in someone's windshield before I shut my eyes and then woke up with you. There's a meaning to all of this, there always is, a plan unfolding. I can't yet know what it is, but I have faith that I will find — Out that we — All will find out in the end. I'm so tired. I want to talk to my wife.

—*Of course. But first I'm hoping you might be able to offer some insight into —*

—What the hell, what the hell. What possible insight could I have? Can't you see that I need a dachshund? Please help me, Henry.

—*Focus, focus, focus. Don't give up on me now.*

—Something went wrong somewhere. That's the extent of my

insight. I did my bit. Now, please. Please. I did everything you told me to. I held up my end. You should've asked me. I'm an expert. At leveraging organizational efficiencies. I need to talk to my wife. I need to tell her. Not to read the letter. I need to tell her I'm a dead man. She's going to see this on TV. She'll think that I'm a part of this. I can't let her know I'm alive. She'll think I ran away. The owl in the forest. DeHoog! DeHoog! The owl was an angel and the angel called my name. Rodney deHoog is a husband, a father, the keeper of an inn. He's not a killer, he never killed, he wouldn't kill someone. He's only ever loved, he's loved too much. He's not a part of this, he was not properly informed. Listen, fellas, fun is fun. I need to talk to Winnifred.

—*Uh-huh. Okay, fuck, all right. [Redacted], hand me the phone.*

—[Inaudible.]

—*Look at him, he's out of it. Too many painkillers, or not enough. Just pop the SIM. Mr. deHoog? Mr. deHoog, can you hear me?*

—Of course I can see you, I'm not deaf.

—*We've got your wife on the line. Here you go.*

—Winnifred? You've got her? Oh, thank God. Winnifred, sugarbuns? Winnifred, I can't hear you. I can't hear her. Are you sure this thing is working?

—*Don't worry, it's a Company phone. She can hear you. We've got her muted for her own safety. So talk. Get it out of your system.*

—Okay, okay. Winnifred? I'm on a special phone so I can't hear you, but it's for the best. I need you just to listen. Darling, there's been an incident at the hotel. I've been terribly injured. I'm being taken to a hospital, but it doesn't look good. My injuries are-are-are-are-are-are-are terrible. If I don't pull through, tell the kids that their dad says *adios*. And-and, oh yes, there's one other thing, sweetheart, that I wanted to tell you, there's a letter in the top drawer of my desk, please just ignore it, toss it out, it's just a —

—*Wait a second, hold on. What letter?*

—It's nothing, I wrote her a letter, explaining.

—*Explaining what? DeHoog? Focus. Explaining what?*

—It's nothing. A confession.

—*A confession, Jesus Christ. Did you say anything about your involvement with us?*

—I told her about my double life. I thought she deserved the truth. I thought I owed her that much. But I was wrong, I can see that now, the truth will only harm us.

—*Fuck. [Redacted], send someone to his house. See if we can clean this up before we have to implement the full procedure. The family shouldn't have to suffer for his idiocy. Tell them we're looking for a letter in the top drawer of his desk. DeHoog, can you hear me? Do you realize you've put your family in a very bad spot? Is your wife home right now? Are your children?*

—Listen, Henry, we must pretend that I'm dead. Winnifred's got my hard drive. I'm surrounded by airplanes, ol' buddy, I'm leaving now, forget about her nudes, I won't tell you her name. We're going to ride our longboat through the swells and the seafoam, we'll land on the shores of Northumbria. The airplanes are here. Hey you. We're leaving now? Hey you, Support, we're leaving now? You, yes yes. You are Support, aren't you? The airplanes are starting to-to-to taxi.

—*We're leaving in a moment, yes.*

—I'm ready, okay. Ready as I'll ever be! Goodbye now, fellas. I'm ready for my big adventure. Welcome to Buttonville hardcore. So long, my Yorkshire pudding. This time tomorrow, I'll be far, far away.

[*Unintelligible comments redacted.*]

END OF TRANSCRIPTION
PREPARED AND SUBMITTED BY: ZHÈNG, Y.L.

C O N F I D E N T I A L [UNDISCLOSED LOCATION] 008957
DEPARTMENT FOR NEA/I
SUBJECT: CORRECTED COPY: ASSET DEBRIEF INTERVIEW

REF: A. [UNDISCLOSED LOCATION] 8957
Classified By: CDA Officer D.J. Rasmussen for reasons: 7.0 (a)–(d).

ASSET ID: "SYSTEMS" [Legal name Ivy Lew]
March 19, 2023 — 01:59 GMT

377 days after Operation Fear and Trembling

—Are we recording? One two, one two. Test test test test. Is this thing working? Yes? It's very important.

Okay, all right. I'm going to tell you a story.

There was a day, last September. I was strolling down the sidewalk, a leafy neighbourhood near my townhouse. I'd just come from counselling with Dr. Jeloni. I'd popped into the pharmacy to get my prescription filled, I didn't have to see her for another two weeks, I was free for fourteen days, such a relief. The air was soft, the smell of gardenia on the breeze. I was going to pop home, kiss my cat, put on some lipstick, and head back out to meet my boyfriend. Austin, his name is, he works for an NGO that delivers vaccines to developing countries. We were meeting in a park, then grabbing a coffee. After that, who knew? Eat some dinner, go see a movie, come home, have sex. I adored him, I was giddy to see him, I was so excited to find out where all this would lead. Austin, the air, the gardenia, the promise of coffee. It was a perfect Friday, you know, one of those. A stranger passed by, a shadow, a blur, the scent of her perfume — I'd smelled that perfume once before, in

Paris, it immediately transported me. A crow was cawing from an eavestrough. I was in love with the world, I never wanted this to end. I had a job that I liked, in a bakery, I had a sweet little flat in a funky part of town, I had everything. I felt like a normal person. And then it hit me.

For a moment I'd forgotten all about them. My son and my husband. The life I'd left behind. Forgotten they'd even existed.

I stopped right there, on the sidewalk, I recall a truck rumbling by, the sound of children playing in the distance. Then the world I so loved spun around madly, like a fairground ride, the Gravitron, and when I woke up two paramedics were lifting me onto a stretcher. Do you understand what I'm saying, the horror of that moment? How easy it was to become someone else, to lose myself, to drift away. What is wrong with me? What kind of monster am I? I don't expect you to answer, it's a rhetorical question. It's a given in your mind that I'm a monster, I'm sure. You're so young, so blond, so certain. When I look at you I smell hayfields and horses. I can tell you're from the south, your accent, it's southern. You don't have to do this, you know.

—*Ma'am?*

—What you're doing. I know what you're going to do. You don't have to do it.

—*Ma'am, I'm afraid I [inaudible].*

—Okay, sure, of course. We'll pretend. La lala lala. Everything is fine and dandy, you and I. By the way, it's Ivy. Call me Ivy. Where are we, anyway? We've been flying for hours.

—*[Inaudible.]*

—Don't you think I have a right to know?

—*Ma'am, [inaudible.]*

—Of course. You don't know anything. Fine. Well, what should we talk about then, before you, before … It's really loud in here, by the way. How can you stand it? Am I being annoying? Am I talking too much? Just tell me, and I'll be sure to talk even more because what do I care anymore? My husband was American, if that makes any difference. Is American, is. He's just like you, but less blond. He has these cute dimples when he doesn't have a beard. He's from Flint, Michigan, the place with the poison water. That's sort of the Midwest, right? You guys could hang out, have a beer, talk football. Right? Am I right? Am I not right when I say that we're all earthlings, that we're all the same deep down, that our differences matter less than what binds us together? Dude? Please? Look at me, please? That whatever agenda, political, whatever, you've grown up with, it's something we can overcome? Yes? My husband, his name is Philip, we met in the Siege of Orgrimmar. Yes? No? Anything? The Siege of Orgrimmar is from an online role-playing game, it's called World of Warcraft. Do you like video games? He shrugs. I know you do. World of Warcraft, you must know this, is a huge alternate world, a fantasy world, the kind you'd love to live inside. Golems and orcs, creatures made of wind. Massive undead insects, ice trolls, carnivorous plants. Thousands of people come together, all across the earth, the real earth, to play it. I was Revinqt of the Drachar realm, he was Shrike of the Sentinels realm. We were Blood Death Knights, both of us, we had that connection. We flirted in the forums. He had this dark sense of humour, not politically correct at all. I hate that, all this woke bullshit. Do you hate that? He made all these subtle references to *Atlas Shrugged*, I loved that. We're both libertarians, the power of the individual. Do you read Ayn Rand? Do you play video games? You must. You look like a video game character in all that Kevlar. You look like you could be in Halo, seriously. That's a compliment, by the way. So I know you play video games, so I know you know what I mean, how intimate it can feel. You get to know the other players, you get to be friends. Maybe you and I could've been friends if we'd met online. I spent my life online before Noah came along, before the inundation of Cheerios and baby shit. It's how you guys recruited me, you dropped that message on 4chan.

—*[Inaudible.]*

—Cicada 3301, I did it the first year.

—*[Inaudible.]*

—The test, you know? The puzzle for nerds, you posted the link online, it was like a scavenger hunt except codey. You're giving me a blank look. You don't know about this? Are you, you must be in a different wing of the Company. The Company. Why do I even call it that anymore? Because I guess I still to this day have no idea who the hell you actually are, are you the CIA? CSIS? FSB, MSS, Mossad, GSD, GRLS? ISI, DGSE, PET, DGI, VDD?

I took the test because, I don't know, I thought I might win something. I'm smart, and determined, and I wanted these traits acknowledged the way real people acknowledge things: with money. Or, failing that, status. But what I got instead was you guys. Not that that's a bad, not that I'm complaining. But that's how I ended up at the King William, working in their half-assed Systems unit. I never understood why you guys placed me there, in that arctic fucking outpost, I was capable of so much more. What could I possibly do there, in that dumbass job?

Until I did understand. That morning I understood, the morning of the operation. It's not like you needed expertise, any monkey could've done what I did, it was something else, something inside me, an intangible quality, you knew who I was and what I stood for, you knew I'd be loyal. And I was. That morning, god. That morning at the hotel. On my break, I'll say it now, I was this close to jumping ship. What have they ever done for you, you owe them nothing, just go, grab your coat, just bolt out that door. But then I caught myself, no, it's not about what they've done or not done, it's about you, your word, what you believe in, you're not that kind of person, you knew there would be sacrifices. And anyway what kind of life will you have if you screw them over, what kind of life will your family have, there is a greater good here, hack off the limb to save the body. So I did, right then and there. I was the limb, and I hacked myself off. I did it on my break, 10:30 a.m., before I got your phone call. I was in the restroom, a stall, weeping into a wad of toilet paper. Some lovely person in the stall next door cleared her throat, asked if I was okay. I'm about to lose everything I've ever loved, I said, my baby's going to grow up without his mother, I said, I found the love of my life in the unlikeliest way, I said, and now I'm going to lose him because I can't say no. Just kidding, I said none of that. What I said was, "Mm-hmm, yeah, I'm fine, thank you." I waited till her toilet flushed, the faucets ran, the hand dryer roared, heels on tile, and I was finally alone. I exited the stall and took stock of myself in the restroom mirror. My nose was snotty, my eyes were pools of blood, it looked like I'd been pepper-sprayed. I was so frustrated with myself. I'd thought I was ready. I wasn't ready. None of us were ready. My husband wasn't ready. He was a brilliant coder, he had a cool job at Ubisoft, he was an amazing Warcraft strategist, and a fun, thoughtful dad, but he was useless at everything else. He had no clue about taxes or when they were due. He left his socks lying everywhere, even once in the freezer. Just six months ago, before a trip out of town for a hospitality conference, I had to teach him how to use the toaster. The fucking toaster. So the thought that Philip might be the sole caregiver of our child, it was terrifying. You're stifling a yawn. Am I boring you? I hope so, it's all I have left, the ability to bore. This sweet blond boy with such an awful task ahead of him, no wonder you've disengaged, how else can you cope? But really, you really, really don't have to do this. You think you do, they told you that you do, but you don't. You can resist, believe me, I know, you can think for yourself. You don't have to do this. Please, don't do this. I know it's a big scary machine you

work for, I know, but you're not just a role, you're not a task, you're
a human being who can think for himself, your role can't contain
who you are, there's so much more of you, you have a mother and a
father and a best friend and a dog maybe, a favourite movie, a song
that gets stuck in your head. And I have all that, too, I'm a human
being, a mother, I'm a mother, my boy's name, I said this, Noah,
he's such a cutie, he reminds me a bit of you, actually, now that I
think about it, sure, around the mouth, and you must know what
that means, to be a mother. You'd do anything to make your baby
happy, you'd sacrifice your own happiness in a heartbeat, your own
life, you'd sacrifice your own life if you thought it would make
your baby's life better. I'm a mother, a human being, and, and, and
an American, too. You didn't know that? You're giving me a look.
I'm literally an American citizen. We're the same. They made me a
dual citizen months ago. But even when I wasn't, even when I was
just a Canadian, I always felt like I was meant to be an American.
I believe what you believe, in freedom, in free enterprise, rational
behaviour, in making your way in this world, no bullshit from big
government. The right to protect your family and your property.
I believe in the power of the individual person, no one can tell
me what to do, the power of that, the power to make your own
decisions, not to be told by some bureaucrat what to do. Your own
decisions. You can do this or that, it's okay, you're a grown-ass
adult. Either or, right? I think you understand me. I think you
understand me. Hold on, what was I talking about?

—*Your husband was a useless [inaudible].*

—Philip, right. Philip. I realized I had to do something. To prepare
him. To take over after I was gone. I enrolled us in cooking class-
es at the local polytech. I taught him how to use the washer and
dryer. I spent hours trying to explain online banking. After what
was it, a year? I concocted a reason to visit my parents, they live
in Vancouver. I told Philip my mom was ill, I had to leave for two

weeks. He was confident, I was less so. I flew away, walked around the seawall, hit the restaurants in Richmond. When I came back, my home looked like a trailer park after a tornado had touched down, furniture pulled from the walls, socks and underwear piled on the kitchen counter. There were scorch marks on the wall above the stove. The cat had started pooping outside the box because the litter was so foul. I locked myself in the bathroom and bawled, Philip was so sweet, so confused, he didn't understand and there was nothing I could tell him. He was less important to me than the contract I signed with you. That was the truth of it. The power of love. Everything we had together, it was nothing in the end, so easily did it crumble and slide away.

I used to log in to the Warcraft forums just to look at his avatar. This was after my collapse on the street, the one I told you about. I'd get weepy, Dr. Jeloni's pills barely kept me upright, so I'd sneak off to the library just before it closed. I'd use their computers. I'd press my finger to his avatar and let him know that I was thinking about him. That I hadn't forgotten. I told him he was a good father, that I believed in him. I read his Warcraft posts, tried to glean information about whether he was okay. I couldn't tell. Truth was, there were very few posts after the day I disappeared, which maybe told me what I needed to know.

I love crying in bathrooms, you can probably tell I do it a lot.

The restroom hadn't been renoed yet. The one in the hotel. Where I had my little breakdown. All the restrooms were getting a full refresh, but this one hadn't been done yet. The new ones upstairs were next-level — waterfall faucets, motion detector bidets — but this one down here was straight out of the nineties. Beige, sponge-painted walls, mildew in the grout. I wasn't ready, none of us were ready. I leaned against the vanity, staring feebly at a vein, a pulsing artery running through the sink, like a prop in a David Cronenberg movie, but when I caught myself and focused my eyes, the vein resolved into a crack, that's all, bisecting the sink, some maintenance guy had filled it with putty. This five-star hotel had seen happier days. I splashed some cold water on my forehead and towelled off and made myself right, then went back to work.

The lobby was busy, there was a breakfast banquet that morning, all kinds of VIPs around, members of Parliament, business bros. I think the mayor might have been there. I'd assumed at the time that the operation had something to do with one of these people. I realize now I was wrong. Why would you care about a member of Parliament? You had bigger balls to bounce, I get it. Carlos Linera, the keynote speaker, that's who you wanted. Yeah, I figured that out after the fact. I could still read the news sites in my exile; as closely as you monitored me, you couldn't keep me away from those. He was a reasonable target, I guess. All the what, the lithium? No, that was Bolivia. It was something else, some strange new thing, a plant. The genome of a plant. Mangoes or ... something else. Something that his country had a lot of. All those precious resources that he was threatening to nationalize. In the name of his people. If they're nationalized, it doesn't help Tesla much, does it? It doesn't help 3M or DuPont. I would've tried to silence him, too, no lie, if I were you guys. Dude is a legit threat.

On my way back to the office, I saw my friend Summer. She was on front desk, talking to a guest. If there was one thing that made me less heartsick about all of this, it was Summer, for real. She was a good person, fun, kind, thoughtful, responsible. I met her at the staff Christmas party like four, four and a half years ago. We'd been assigned to the same table, someone from HR thought it was good policy to force strangers to eat together. Dinner was over, speeches had been spoken, unending bullcrap from deHoog, our manager of operations, and his minions about our relentless pursuit of excellence, of exceeding expectations, which was his way of saying they were planning to cut staff and make the survivors work harder for less money. Now it was the wine portion of the evening. Some people I knew from Catering were up on the stage, singing karaoke. Fleetwood Mac, Simple Minds. Pop shit from the seventies and eighties. "Don't You Forget About Me." They had a disco ball. Diamond shards shooting across the walls. Summer was hilarious. She kept making jokes about deHoog, what a perv he was, how he stared at her in the hallways. "Can you imagine kissing that face?" she said, and mimed choking down vomit. She was tough, in control, but sad, too, I could tell, appealingly sad, not scary sad, there was something in her eyes, I liked her right away. And Philip liked her, too, I saw, although in a different way. We were watching the karaoke, I glanced over at him, I caught him peeking at her boobs. Which stung me at first, naturally, but a split second later I thought, Ah-ha! You know? Here it is. Maybe this is the solution. So at the end of the night I tell her we should hit a patio sometime when it warms up, for sangria. She smiles, says great. And that's how I started it, setting up my husband with his new wife.

The look on your face. What? You're giving me a look. You have to understand, this was four years ago, I'd already been waiting for years at that point, not knowing anything, no idea when I'd be activated or what I'd be forced to do. I'd stare up at the ceiling, any given night, three in the morning, Philip beside me in bed, think-ing, one day this will end, this great love, and one day my baby won't have his mother. Can you even guess how that feels, how it eats away at the brain?

I couldn't have imagined at that time that one day they'd be all but erased, I'd be lying in a bed three time zones away with some other man I felt like I'd known forever. If you'd met him, Austin, I mean, you'd understand why. He's so solid, so strong. He was with me that night. The night I realized I was being monitored. We'd been watching an old movie, Stanley Kubrick, *The Killing*,

it was called, I hadn't seen it yet. Black and white. This was last
October, I remember the smell of the air, the ocean. Austin's teeth
were stained with merlot. A strange sound, a buzzing, was coming
from the floor lamp, like a hornet was trapped inside its base. I
paused the TV and turned off the lamp, the lamp still buzzed. We
frowned at each other, we debated the mystery sound, whether
we should investigate. "Maybe it's a sonic attack," Austin said. He
was kidding, but a queasy unease crept over me. At length, Austin
unplugged it, still the thing buzzed. I'll never forget his expression, the sweet curious consternation, this puzzle to be figured out.
He picked it up, turned it over, I went to find the screwdriver.
Inside, when we got it open, we discovered a black box tacked
to the top side. I plucked it out, turned it over and around. It
said *DOWN7* on one edge. I remembered this, of course, from
the YouTube channel that triggered the operation. I had a little
freak-out then, but mostly managed to hide it from Austin. Maybe
I let a groan slip out, I can't be certain. Austin wanted to google
it, to figure out what this buzzing box was supposed to be, but of
course I talked him out of it. We resumed the movie, and I stared
thoughtlessly at the television until it was finished. Next morning,
I got up early, went straight to the library, and confirmed what I'd
suspected. You'd been listening to me. And it's not even that I was
all that surprised. Was it you, was it the NSA, was it the DGI? And
how about you, are you Mossad? Are you a Proud Boy? And what
about Austin? I'm not stupid, I guessed the plan; you wanted to in-
tegrate me, keep me happy, keep me occupied till you could decide
what to do with me. Was Austin part of your integration strategy?
The thought had occurred to me, even at home, even with him in
bed. But then I'd look at his chest, the amount he works out, it
pays off, believe me, and I wouldn't care anymore. Maybe he was
FSB, ISI. Maybe he was deep cover for someone else. I know I'll
never know. HUMINT, SIGINT, I'm in tech, I'm a geek, I know

there are no limits on the data you can gather, but there are limits, there are limits on what you can understand about a human. There are things deep down, shadows and fragments, disembodied voices whispering information that no amount of digging can extract. At the King William I could access all kinds of data, I could piece it together, credit card numbers, loyalty points, addresses and phone numbers and room service orders, I could draw you a picture of somebody's life, their habits and predilections. From that you could interpolate or extrapolate, you could apply exotic algorithms, and what would you learn? You'd never know another person's heart, you'd never divine the connections, the forces that bind us together. The person I spoke to on the phone the day of the operation, the one who who gave me my instructions. She had a mother and a father, maybe a husband and a kid, maybe a cat, a favourite top, she had a childhood that never could have prepared her for her conversation with me. But somehow there we were, at 11:30 that morning. "Ivy, use your administrator login to access the CRS," she told me. "Query the Reservations module for a booking in one of three names: Margaretha MacLeod, Yoshiko Kawashima, Elsbeth Schragmüller. Write that down. If-slash-when you get a hit, compare and confirm this with the entries in the profile module. The booking should have originated in Ecuador, but perhaps not. Possibly Russia, possibly another pariah state."

At 1:45 p.m., I sat down at my station and logged in to the CRS. There were two other people in the office at that point. Sharon, our team leader, she was perpetually crabby, but in a fun way, she was at the servers, and Tomas, he was a child straight out of college, suit two sizes too big, he was answering a ticket from one of the other departments. I queried Reservations for the names, got a hit for Elsbeth Schragmüller. A room had been booked with a credit card issued by an Ecuadorian bank. The booking was for room 1801, I made a mental note. I got up. I slid over to the filing cabinet by the main door. This was where we kept a box of untouched RFIDs, the key cards for the suites; it was a failsafe in case the readers on front desk went offline. I glanced behind me — Sharon was immersed in the servers, making ticks on a clipboard, murmuring under her breath; Tomas was clacking away at his laptop. I grabbed a key card, beelined back to my station, plugged the card into my reader, and charged it with the suite number, 1801. There was redundant security for the Royal Suites, no duplicate keys were allowed without triggering an alarm; I overrode that. Whoever possessed this, whether friend or foe, would have unimpeded access to the suite and whatever or whoever was inside.

The whole thing took maybe ninety seconds, maybe less, but when I got up to leave, there was Sharon's pale round face not five steps away, as if she'd been beamed there. She was frowning at me. "Ivy, what are you doing?" she said.

"I'm sorry?" I said.

"This Wednesday after work?" Sharon said. "What are you doing?"

"I don't know," I said. "Why?" My face felt poached, as if her gaze were a heat lamp. My voice felt foreign, far away, someone else was speaking the words.

"I have a four-hour meeting that afternoon," she said. "Channel Management and PMS Integration. I'm pretty sure I'll need a cocktail or three afterward."

"Okay," I said, "sounds perfect," I said, "count me in," I said, I'll be long gone by then, three time zones away, in a bar by the bay, sunlight sparkling on the waves, but I'll drink a toast in your honour, I said, no I didn't, but I should have. I smiled, I said sure, I went back to my station, stuck the RFID card into a sleeve, tucked in the note they'd told me to include. Then logged off the CRS and attempted to think. I was damp, in my collar, in my armpits, all over. The soles of my feet had the sweats. I was dying to splash some more water on my face, but there wasn't time. I checked the clock on my laptop, 1:50. I had someplace to be. It's so loud in here. It feels like I'm yelling. Can you hear me all right?

—*[Inaudible.]*

—I said I had someplace to be! I'll speak louder! I had someplace to be, but then again I always do, I'm never where I'm supposed to be, always in between. I've been washing up on these little islands of peace and comfort where I can rest my head and catch my breath until it's time to wade back out into the torment. That's how I've come to think of Toronto, anyway. My life there, with Philip and Noah. I knew the time would come when I'd have to strand them there, on that island, which would for the rest of time exist for me only in amber, in a memory, not real, just something that might have happened once. His new wife, Summer, ha, she'd be his reality, not me, I'd be just a puzzle, a question that would never be answered. I asked her out for sangria. We talked, a lot a lot, we got a little drunk, I plied her with booze and asked her questions. Where are you from. What's your family like. Are you seeing anyone. She had a boyfriend, Steve, I wasn't troubled by that, he was just a man, mine was better. Nothing that Summer said raised any red flags. She was from a tiny little hamlet near the top of Lake Superior, you've never heard of it. Her parents were hippie homesteaders. In the summers, she said, she had wandered the woods, a forest nymph, picking wintergreen and wild blueberries. She gave names to the foxes that wandered across their property. It sounded so lovely. In winter she snowshoed, she slept in the glow of a wood stove.

Did you know it takes two hundred years for the water that feeds Lake Superior to make its way to Niagara Falls? She'd come all this way.

I saw how she'd looked at my husband, the side-eye — I saw how they'd looked, or avoided looking, at each other. It was all good. The first thing I did, if I remember, was to invite her up to Markham for dinner. It was a trek for her on transit, so I sent Philip downtown to pick her up. We ate Tibetan, *thukpa bhathuk*, we watched an episode of *Doctor Who*, then Philip drove her home.

It wasn't that long until we were meeting more regularly. For drinks after work, Second City, TIFF, one thing or another. She had an unrestrained, almost maniacal laugh, she loved how absurd and unlikely the world could be. She loved stand-up comedy and *Twin Peaks* and floaty synth music sung by monotone Swedes. She possessed an uncomplicated affection for Ikea cod roe spread, the kind that comes in tubes, you squeeze it onto crackers. But there was something else to her, too, I don't know, it's hard to explain, not a sadness. A graveness, a gravity. There were times I'd see her staring off, a little fold between her eyebrows. She was staring inward, I guess, at something that had happened to her maybe, or something that might be on its way.

She said to me once, "You're so dumb when you're young, you make such stupid decisions." We were in the car, on the way to an orchard to pick apples. "You're angry," she said, "you're jealous, you're consumed by nihilism. A moment of vulnerability alters your life forever."

Well. As you can imagine, I pressed her on this, but she wouldn't say anything else. Just this vague, sad statement. It worried me a bit, it followed me around. After dinner, washing the dishes, I'd stop and wonder. But I chose to ignore it in the end. Everyone has a past, she was allowed hers. We went to a Jays game, we went to a free concert at Yonge-Dundas Square, my big evening in the city. On a Saturday I took her with us to Pacific Mall. We had lunch, we wandered through the food stalls. It was lovely, so lovely. She was my friend, my replacement, my great hope. She babysat a couple times, she was so good with Noah. Then one night, after a dinner, I had Philip drive her home. He took longer than usual, a lot longer. It should have taken him an hour, it took him two hours. He was quiet when he got home, went straight to the bathroom and brushed his teeth. I didn't ask. I wanted to so badly, I needed to know, but what could I say? He told me traffic was a nightmare on the 401. An accident, a tractor-trailer, something like that. He wouldn't look me in the eyes. I knew, I'm not stupid, it was obvious, but I wished I had that little extra, the proof, the proof.

I couldn't sleep that night. I stared into the ceiling static taking turns feeling heartbroken and elated. My succession plan was working. My beautiful man, my beautiful man, my beautiful man. Had slept with someone else. I fell asleep. Had strange, fitful dreams, of displacement and loss, of longing and transformation, of one strange afternoon at work, and when I woke up I was nuzzling the neck of an entirely different man. My husband was Doctor Who. "I love you so much," Austin said. "I love you so goddamn much." He's so vulnerable when he's just waking up, so sleepy and pliant. I reached down and fondled him. "Gimme some of this," I said, "then I'll make you some eggs."

This was a month ago, Jesus, it was the last day I saw him, a Sunday, so lazy, we had brunch and did the crossword and went for coffee and then nine hours later, after Austin had gone home and I'd gone to bed, a squadron of Dreadlords stormed into my bedroom with their tactical flashlights drawn, screaming at me to get up and get dressed. They dragged me to their van, then drove me into some vast industrial space on the outskirts of town. We pulled into a warehouse, it was empty but for one chair. They sat me in the chair. And there I stayed, two days I think, I can't be sure, they trained their floodlights on me, played the Meow Mix jingle over and over at brain-melting volume, meow meow meow meow, I've memorized the lyrics, I can sing them if you'd like, over and over until I couldn't form a thought, no food, no water, an ice cube every hour, until it all just stopped, and the men disappeared. A period of peaceful, terrifying quiet. A door opened, then closed with a metallic thwack. Footsteps echoed on the concrete floor. Then a man knelt down in front of me, a soft voice.

"You've soiled yourself," he said.

I tried to care, I couldn't. He said, "I guess you know why you're here." I did, but I wasn't going to make his job any easier. He said his name was [Redacted]. He said, "Lookit, Ivy, we know what happened. We know what happened, we'd like to know why. That's all. No judgment. Walk me through it. We'd like to know how and why. You'll save yourself a whole lot of unnecessary grief, and you'll be doing me a great favour. My boss, she's not happy with me right now. I'd like to change that if I could. Can you help a brother out?"

He smiled at me, I saw teeth, I tried to keep his face in focus. He was handsome, he looked a bit like *The Wire*, that guy, McNulty, only blurry at the edges. He wore a short-sleeve dress shirt, pale-blue Dockers, deck shoes. "Help a brother out," he said, as if we were a family. Who knows, maybe we were. Powerful forces had drawn us together, money and, and, and domination, control, protection. Ancient forces that found new forms. The World of Warcraft. Raids and sieges and deathwings and old gods and night elves and rave mobs and plaguelands and tainted scars and emerald nightmares and hordes and cataclysms and doomguard bosses. We were bound together with ropes made out of our own vile natures.

He smiled with benevolence, put a hand on my shoulder. "This is for the future," he said. "You can help us avoid this in the future. You can help us save lives. If you help us," he said, "you can help yourself, too. More than that," he said, "you can help all the people you love the most." He smiled, so kindly he was, so helpful. He smiled so wide that his skin rolled back to show me the hellhound underneath, the fangs, the blood-red eyes.

I tried to think. They'd removed thought from my repertoire, but I tried. If I gave them what they wanted, would that help me or hurt me? Maybe they were bluffing. Maybe this was a test, a loyalty

thing. I held off. For two more days I said nothing. I pissed myself, I sat in my own excrement. Then my new friend [Redacted]
came back with an envelope, manila, like Mona's in Toronto. He
plucked out some photos, spread them on the floor in front of me.
The first one was Noah. He was in a playground near our house.
The second was Philip and Noah at the mall, eating fried noo-
dles in the food court. The third was Noah asleep in his bed, his
little stuffed bunny tucked under his arm. I didn't need to see the
fourth, the fifth, the sixth, or the seventh.

"How did you know it was me?" I said.

He gave me an impish look, shook his head and studied his
shoes. "You just told me," he said.

That morning, after the Twitter. The morning of the operation.
You can judge me if you want, I need to be judged. That morning, after the Twitter and the YouTube and the OpenPuff, I got
dressed. I did my hair and put on my face and ate some gluten-free
toast. My nails, I noticed, as I choked down the toast, were flaw-
less. I'd just gotten them done, a metallic periwinkle shellac mani.
So at least I had that. The words, the words, going through my
head. I checked the freezer, made sure they had food for the week.
Greetings from Copenhagen, the gardens are green. I put some
fresh towels in the cupboard, where I hoped Philip would find
them. Greetings from Copenhagen. I made a note on the fridge:
hydro due March 15. I went up to Noah's room, pressed my hand
against his door, it didn't burn or sting. I felt nothing. How could I
not feel anything? I put my hand on the knob. Still nothing. Such
relief. I'd killed that part of my heart. I would be able to function,
I wouldn't be doubled over with grey mindless agony, I could do
my job. I didn't go inside, didn't push it. To see him in bed with
his bunny, to kiss his little nose, no. I preferred feeling nothing.
Does that make me bad? I tiptoed downstairs, pinned a note to
the fridge to pick up dishwasher detergent, then out to the car and

into the traffic surge, the endless commute, all the drivers dreaming, humans encased in our machines, wishing we could be freed of all this bullshit.

At work I kind of lost it. A moment of rage, I couldn't help it, I was trapped inside the moment, it told me what to do. It was 1:55, I'd just left the Systems office. The key card for Suite 1801 sat in the breast pocket of my blazer, just above my heart. I could feel it there, glowing, like some radioactive isotope, this token of my sacrifice, burning through my chest. I was standing in the corridor waiting for an elevator. Nervous, angry, jealous, happy, all of these things. An elderly couple approached. The way they looked at me, they telegraphed their neediness. "Miss?" the man said. "Miss? Where is the manager of this hotel? We want to know where his office is located." The old guy, his eyes were wet and imploring. He spoke loudly, slowly, like he doubted I knew English. "Down the hall, first right, can't miss it," I said. "We are unhappy with the state of this hotel," he said. "We have come here many times previous to this, and will not be returning based on today's experiences." The elevator doors opened, I stepped toward them.

"Miss," he said, "I'm speaking to you."

I whipped around and stared them down, those orcs in Gucci eyewear. "Don't be so fucking weak," I said. "You're having a bad day. You're not the only one. There are a few of us. So shut the fuck up and act like an adult." I smiled sweetly and backed into the elevator. The doors closed, their faces were priceless, staring at me like I was a distempered raccoon, like I'd just bit them, like my virus was pulsing through their bloodstreams. The doors reopened onto the convention floor. It was quiet, no conventions had been booked given the big one on the main floor, and no staff that I could hear. The faint lemony smell of disinfectant. I pulled the access card from my pocket. Inhaled through the nose, exhaled through the mouth, three times, to calm myself. I did not think about Noah, I did not think about Noah, I was doing this for him, for the greater good, for him, he'd be so proud of me if only he knew, the strength it must have taken for his mommy to do this, what courage, what resolve, I was a soldier, a superman, and my only consolation in the face of this great desolate act was that my son would still have a mother, not his real one, no, but a wonderful mother nonetheless, someone who would teach him how to be a human in this, the grimmest of all possible worlds.

The person on the phone told me to be at the convention floor women's facilities at 2:15 exactly. I got there early, staked it out behind a potted palm. At 2:05, I saw movement, someone coming down the hall, a woman. When she came closer I realized the woman was Summer Johnson — of all people, Summer fucking Johnson. The worst timing, right? She moved with obvious resolve. When she reached the restroom, she paused, surveyed her surroundings, before opening the door and entering. It was weird that she was here, in addition to being massively inconvenient. Reservations has its own staff room, with toilet. But probably she just needed some privacy. So I waited. Waited some more. She didn't exit. I glanced at my watch, there were five minutes to hand-off. If she were in there while I did this thing, it would be, I don't know, awkward? Somehow? Plus what was she even doing there in the first place? I couldn't take it. I left my post and followed her inside, expecting to find her at one of the sinks, touching up her lip gloss, for front of house you're allowed only a basic nude. But she wasn't there, no one was there, no one at all. What the fuck, right? So I squatted, peered under the stall dividers, and that's when I saw the long stockinged legs and the comfortable flats, in the third of five stalls. The middle stall.

It took me a moment. A moment of disbelief, a moment in which I didn't breathe. Until it came to me, the undeniable fact, as much as I wanted to deny it: Summer was my contact, she was part of this, whatever this was, this misery, this manipulation. My god, you monsters.

—*[Inaudible.]*

—Well, when I was able, I stood again and exited the restroom. I'm not sure how long that took. I attempted thought. I'd trusted her, you know, she should have known better. How could she do this? How could she fuck my husband, then abandon my son, and destroy my family? But then again, of course it wasn't really her, was it? It was the Company. The poor thing, she had fallen into the same trap that I had. This was my moment of clarity, Wise Mind overpowering Emotional Mind. You were the ones who orphaned my son, not her. A human life means nothing to a Board of Directors, it's just a mathematical equation, VSL, the value of statistical life, how do we keep the shareholders happy?

The corridor was attempting a funhouse floor trick, it swung back and forth, side by side; I grabbed at the first thing I could reach, a potted palm, to keep myself upright. Bile was roiling up from the deepest, blackest part of me, a maternal rage. I wanted to gnaw away your neck, to bite off your balls, to yank out your liver while you watched. I can't recall now even choosing to do it, I just did it. So many of the big decisions in our life, we're just fated to make them, screw free will. I remember running wildly, I must have looked like a Worgen, for real, back down the hallway to the elevators, and up to the Systems office.

Why, you might ask, did I return to the Systems office? You're not asking, you don't care. But I'll tell you.

I returned to the office to fuck you with an Elementium Poleaxe. Sorry.

Not sorry.

I buzzed in and rushed to my station and no one even noticed, that's the perk of working with people on the spectrum. And then I reprogrammed the card so that whoever it was who tapped it on the lock of Suite 1801 would set off security, fire, and overhead sprinklers.

Then I flailed my way back to the convention floor women's facilities, took a moment to settle myself, and opened the door. My blouse was wet with perspiration, I could barely catch my breath. I stepped to the middle stall. Considered for a moment whether to say something, you know, like, "Sweetheart, please don't go through with this, please." I could almost see her inside there, my dearest friend Summer, bleary-eyed, squatting on the toilet seat, as though I could see through the stall door. I wanted so badly to hug her, to tell her it would all be okay. But I said nothing, because it wouldn't be okay, for either of us. I kneeled down and flipped the key card onto the tiles and left the restroom and left the hotel and left the express train and left the airport and left my family and flew away like a peregrine, never to return.

I had no idea what you were planning, but whatever it was, you were fucked, and I'm the one who fucked you. It was me. And I'm not sorry. And I'd do it all again. So go ahead, if you feel like you have to, open that box on the wall, and enter the passcode, and open that hatch. Throw my sorry bones into the stratosphere, watch me drop. Thirty thousand feet, that's so cruel. I'll explode on the surface of the water, you know that, right, I'll be chum for the sharks. Will you listen to me scream? I did it out of love, you understand love, right? You love your mother, you love your dad, you love your dog and your best friend and your girlfriend or your boyfriend or whoever it is. We're earthlings, we're human Americans, we're in this together, don't let them come between us. It wasn't treason, it wasn't sabotage, it was love, the anger that could only come from love, and you do understand love, you do, you're getting up, please don't get up, you can resist, they make it seem like it's not you, you're just the muscle, it's them, they make the decisions, but it is you, it is you, you can do differently, you don't have to do what these blood elves tell you to do, let's talk a little more, you and me, let's hash this thing out, come to some conclusions, let's whine and complain, let's save the world, please stop pushing those buttons, we can do this, you and me, I'm not going to help you, I'm not standing up, no, I'm not, I'm not going to stand, you're hurting me, you don't have to do this, believe me, I know, believe me, no, you're hurting me, believe me, no, you're hurting me, believe me.

[*Unintelligible comments redacted.*]

END OF TRANSCRIPTION
PREPARED AND SUBMITTED BY: RASMUSSEN, D.J.

Nadja,

So there you have it. Operation Fear and Trembling.

A short postface to the shocking events just described. Starting with some gripes. Who named this operation? Was it Berger? The son of a bitch always fancied himself an aesthete. What was his mania for themed operations? Kierkegaard, blah blah blah, Greetings from Copenhagen, please, come on. First thing moving forward, if I have any say, we're going to lose all this cutesy shit and get back to fundamentals, hire some competent business analysts to do a workflow assessment. I'm certain this is Berger's work. Such a colossal dumbass, that guy. May he rest in peace.

And by the way, who signed off on a nerve agent? In a chutney jar, no less? Were we staging a grand opera or something? That's state-sponsored nonsense, that's trying to get noticed. We should have just gone in there with a mouse gun, one of those little Ruger LCP .380s, and shot the great Mr. Linera in the orbital cavity while he was having a shower. No fuss, no muss, a quick wipe down for the cleaners. Instead, our poorly vetted third-party vendor panics in the face of mild adversity. (Did anyone check this asshole's references?) The nerve agent gets spilled, Linera lives, and his two bodyguards go down the old-fashioned way: in a hail of bullets. Not even deHoog, whose hapless disposition might suggest such an outcome, got a taste of the good stuff: his post-mortem chemistry was clean. A total waste of resources.

And while I'm at it, how many hotels have we staffed, exactly? I'm curious. I know about the buildings in Berlin, in L.A., London, of course. Cape Town, maybe? Am I misremembering? The casino in Macau, the golf resort in Florida. What else? We are everywhere, aren't we? Is the Board even in charge anymore, or has it relented completely to the activist shareholders?

Rant over, with apologies.

A quick summary of the events that followed the operation, offered here for the historical record, and for my own peace of mind:

Carlos Linera, being alive, being not dead due to our operational failure, went on, two months after the operation, to become president of his country, democratically elected by a plurality of his fellow countrymen. One has to appreciate the irony of this, that Linera's landslide was in no small part due to Operation Fear and Trembling. Our attempt on his life stoked the outrage of his people and turned him into a national hero. Not exactly the outcome we were aiming for.

One of Linera's first acts as president was to nationalize the country's rare earth metals, along with its crystal-clear mineral water reserves and its guavasteen crops, the exploitation of which would allow his country to build roads and schools and hospitals and to become a force in the international economy.

In synchrony with this act, many thousands of miles away, a swarm of furious traders on the floor of the New York Stock Exchange watched the stock price of several technology companies, upstream energy concerns, and private equity firms take a deep dive into the toilet. Spooky action at a distance. Rotate a photon in England, a different photon rotates in France.

Among those affected was a little-known but handsomely backed biotech start-up called GuaVax Ltd., which had spent several years hyping and had staked much of its future earnings upon its development of plantibody serums. What are these? Well, let me lay it out for posterity. Since Covid-19 swept its ultraviolet wand over the earth, exposing for all to see the douchebags and sociopaths who had overrun and debased it, disaster capitalists everywhere smelled opportunity. Plagues are the future, et cetera.

And so the smart money flooded into any and all of the immuno-
therapeutical agents that might deliver a decent return on investment. Enter the plantibody.

Plantibodies are the Frankensteinian fusion of plant and human
DNA; in the language of the venture capitalists, they're versatile
and scalable and effective against a variety of immunological insults, i.e., coronaviruses and what-have-yous. For reasons that only
Zeus himself understands, the plant whose chemical components
fuse most effectively with human DNA is the humble guavasteen,
that delicious staple of the fruit smoothie. And not just any old
guavasteen either, but only those that are cultivated in a very particular part of the world. Which part of the world? You guessed it,
that which is now overseen by one Carlos Linera. Something about
the composition of the rainforest soil. This was soil that GuaVax
Ltd. and its shadowy investors very much wanted to occupy, in a
perpetual sort of way, in the manner of the great rubber barons of
yore. But now, with the election of Carlos Linera's ACP Party, an
elected government, not a Western enterprise, is in control of said
soil and all of the magical potions that might arise from it.

As you're well aware, this was a problem for us, because GuaVax
Ltd. was our client. Was, I repeat, was our client. The very one, in
fact, that had commissioned Operation Fear and Trembling. The
failure of the operation voided our contract with GuaVax Ltd.,
leaving us in a vulnerable position, as the revenues that our plucky
little company had depended upon for its continued ability to
thrive were suddenly gone, poof. Which brings us to today. Here
we are, under new ownership, a hedge fund naturally, and you
and me now answerable to effete little Nasdaq knobs who have no
appreciation for our delicate work.

"Merchants have no country," a fella once said.

What's trickled down to me in the last few days from our inter-
im management team is a desire to mop up any spills. Operation

Fear and Trembling is a New Coke–level fuck-up that the share-holders want no part of. Most of our loose ends have been easy enough to tie off, and if I'm not misremembering, most were dealt with preemptively, in anticipation of a hostile takeover.

Most, I say.

One, however — one is outstanding. And I'm told must be our priority for at least Q1 and likely through Q3. Can you guess which?

Don't answer. I'll just tell you.

Summer Johnson has gone missing, we've been unable to lo-cate her. Last week we sent Company operatives to her flat, but she was nowhere to be found, and the place looked to have been hastily vacated. Clothing still in the closet, leftovers rotting in the fridge. Someone, presumably Summer Johnson herself, had dis-covered and pulled our bugs from all the various light switches and electrical outlets; our cameras were snipped and dropped on the floor where we'd find them. As a consequence, we have no audio or video of her, nothing, from something like August onward. Her landlady — a civilian, not on our payroll — said she hadn't seen her for months.

I don't know what to say, Nadja. I'd love to blame this on or-ganizational rightsizing, but we both know it runs deeper than that.

We have eyeballs on the ex-boyfriend's place in Toronto. He's moved apartments since her disappearance, and in recent days seems to have found some new companionship, quite a bit of it actually, none of whom is the party in question. I don't know how much longer we can maintain this level of surveillance; there's no accommodation for it in the revised quarterly budget. So for now, I guess, Summer Johnson has gone dark.

I'm mixed on this, Nadja, you won't be surprised, as I am am-bivalent about most things in this world. In my middle age, I've forsworn certainty. Certainty is a plague upon the populace; it corrupts and divides. And so I'm torn between the interests of the Company, which is to say "my interests," and my investment in the adventures this young lady is having. I wish her a long and happy one, what can I say? She reminds me of the guy I used to be, the aspiring painter in that long-ago city. It's romantic. I'm jealous.

Enough. See you at the Board meeting. It's scheduled for 7 a.m. (not a typo) next Monday morning. Try not to drink too much the night before. It really doesn't help, believe me.

Until then.
Nestor

ACKNOWLEDGEMENTS

The first person to thank is my editor, Russell Smith, who reached into a black hole and pulled out a book. Thank you, Russell, for your guidance, your patience, and your humour.

I'm grateful to my editorial consultant, Joel Pylyshyn, for his insight, generous intelligence, and hilarious, decades-long friendship.

I am in debt to these true-blue humans, for encouraging, entertaining, consoling, or just generally keeping the author upright and semi-functional at one time or another during the long gestation of *Seven Down*: Alex Boyd, Andrew Daley, Bonnie Bowman, Jonathan Dewdney, Liz Howard, Margie Borschke, Phil Saunders, and, of course, Waneta Storms (and Avie and Lou).

Love to my family for their nonstop support: Wells, Donna, Janet, Jim, John, Tina, Bob, Donna, and, especially, Sharon Lea and Tom, for feeding, watering, and wisely counselling me during the plague. Reluctantly tolerated hugs to my two marvellous pretzels, Wallace and Ellroy.

Thanks to Catherine Bush, an early reader and the coordinator of the Creative Writing MFA at the University of Guelph, where this story was first conceived.

Huge gratitude to the next-level earthlings of Dundurn Press: Scott Fraser, Jenny McWha, Sara D'Agostino, Laura Boyle, and Kristina Jagger, as well as Catharine Chen and Shari Rutherford. Thanks to all of you!

ABOUT THE AUTHOR

David Whitton is the author of *The Reverse Cowgirl*, a story collection. His short fiction has appeared in a number of journals and anthologies, including *Darwin's Bastards*, *Best Canadian Stories*, and *The Journey Prize Stories*, and he is a graduate of the University of Guelph's Creative Writing MFA program. David lives in Toronto.